'Oh, God,'

Cass swallowed.

Gifford gazed a ~~~~~~~~~~~~~~~. What seemed like hours went by before he spoke again.

'Why didn't you tell me? I have a son, and yet for nine months you keep quiet about him. You don't bother to inform me that I'm a father. You conceal his existence. How dare you?' he raged.

Jack began to cry. 'Shh, popcorn, shh.' Cass rubbed the baby's back and rocked him against her. 'I did tell you,' she said, speaking in a fervent whisper. 'I wrote two letters.' Her chin tilted. Her blue eyes burned into his. 'Remember?'

'I never received any letters.'

'You didn't tear them up?'

'No.'

'Are you sure?' she challenged.

'Positive,' he grated.

'Well, I sent them. Shh,' Cass said again, rocking the baby. 'I sent the first—'

'Leave it,' Gifford interjected. 'We can't talk now. Come to the villa tomorrow morning.' He frowned at the bawling child. 'And bring him.'

Elizabeth Oldfield's writing career started as a teenage hobby, when she had articles published. However, on her marriage the creative instinct was diverted into the production of a daughter and son. A decade later, when her husband's job took them to Singapore, she resumed writing and had her first romance accepted in 1982. Now hooked on the genre, she produces an average of three books a year. They live in London, and Elizabeth travels widely to authenticate the background of her books.

Recent titles by the same author:

RELUCTANT
FATHER!

BY
ELIZABETH OLDFIELD

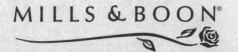

MILLS & BOON®

First published in Great Britain 1997
Harlequin Mills & Boon Limited,
Eton House, 18-24 Paradise Road, Richmond, Surrey TW9 1SR

© Elizabeth Oldfield 1997

ISBN 0 263 80607 3

Set in Times Roman 10½ on 11½ pt.
01-9802-50268 C1

Printed and bound in Great Britain
by Mackays of Chatham PLC, Chatham

CHAPTER ONE

THERE was the rasping of a chair on wooden floorboards.

Cassandra Morrow sighed, uncrossed her eyes and let the held-taut strand of wheat-blonde hair drop back over her brow. She made a face at the Afghan-hound reflection which she saw in the mirror. Her haircut must wait. The noise signalled that a customer had arrived—an unexpected, out-of-the-blue customer whom—frustratingly—she would have to send away.

Jettisoning the scissors, she went to peer around the open door of the ladies' restroom. Her glance swept across the thatch-roofed, open-sided restaurant. Yes, a dark-haired man in a navy polo shirt and faded denims was sitting at a table at the far end. With his chair half turned to accommodate the stretch of his long legs, he was gazing out at the sun-sparkled sapphire of the Indian Ocean.

'Hard luck, mister,' Cass murmured regretfully, 'you're about two hours too early.'

She hoicked the blonde straggles out of her eyes, tugged at her pink skinny-rib top and hastily thumbnailed two dots of dried something—baby muesli?—from her crumpled khaki shorts. A trickle of perspiration was wiped from her chin. The Forgotten Eden guest house and restaurant might not be the London Savoy with its Grill Room, but she didn't want to look too disreputable.

Closing the door of the sparkling-clean restroom behind her, Cass threaded a path between the cluster of batik-clothed tables. Her smooth brow crinkled. She

5

hated the idea of turning down trade, so why should she? The opening hours were not carved in stone. Besides, plugging in the percolator or prising off a bottle top was easy. No catering skills were required there. Nor for depositing a slice of home-made coconut cake on a plate.

And if her service was extra obliging and ultra-efficient perhaps the customer might feel inclined to return for a meal on some other occasion. It would be good to hear the cash till ring.

'Good morning, sir,' she said, smiling a bright, welcoming smile. 'Strictly speaking the restaurant doesn't open for non-residents until twelve—and today we're serving one of our specialities which is a delicious Creole-style fish casserole. However, I'd be very happy to get you a cup of coffee or a glass of cold beer if you—'

As the man turned his head to look up at her, her smile collapsed and the sentence unravelled into silence. A stunned silence. She had heard of shock rocking people back on their heels, and now she felt herself sway. The man gazing up with narrowed grey eyes was Gifford Tait, hot-shot business tycoon, Mr Don't-Fence-Me-In, and—her mind flew to the baby who had been wheeled off earlier in his buggy—the errant father of her nine-month-old son.

Reaching blindly out, Cass clutched at the back of the nearest available chair. Once she had doted on his looks and every aspect about him, so why hadn't she recognised the head of thick, dark hair, the broad, flat shoulders, his air of calm male confidence? Because she had long ago abandoned any idea that Gifford might instigate a get-together and it had never even entered let alone crossed her mind that he would seek her out in the Seychelles!

How had he known where to find her? Why, after

eighteen months when he had remained resolutely in-communicado, had he decided to make the long-haul flight? she wondered, a blizzard of questions starting to swirl in her head. A fit of conscience about his offspring must have finally struck—but what did he have in mind?

To make coochy-coo, forgive-me noises over the cot? Or simply to check that the baby was thriving? Maybe the thought of ten tiny fingers and ten tiny toes had inspired a desire to become a dedicated parent. Her blue eyes darkened. No—never that.

Letting go of the chair, Cass stood up straight. Whatever form it took, his show of interest had come cruelly and callously *late*. If he expected her to toss out the red carpet or blubber her gratitude, he could think again. She was no damsel in distress about to press thankful kisses to the feet of her saviour.

And how dared he arrive unannounced? What right had he to saunter into the restaurant and take her by surprise? And pick a time when she was pink-faced from floor-mopping, hound-dog shaggy and out of shape. Furtively, she pulled in her stomach. It wasn't that she wanted to impress him—no chance—but if she had looked halfway decent she would have felt more poised and less wrong-footed. Not so disastrously thrown.

'I don't—' she started, with some heat, but he got there first.

'What the hell are you doing here?' Gifford demanded, in a low, gravelly voice with an American accent.

As he had flown from the States to Europe, and on from Europe to the middle reaches of the Indian Ocean, he had been thinking about Cassandra Morrow. He had been thinking about her and their past involvement with an irritating frequency for God knew how long. His lips compressed. Thinking about her always made him uneasy and provoked regrets—and to be confronted by her now felt as if someone had punched him hard and low in the gut.

Cass blinked. She had, she realised, got it wrong. All wrong. His question, plus the narrowed gaze, showed that he was just as astonished to see her as she was to see him. And a tightness around his mouth indicated he was not exactly jumping for joy, either. Gifford Tait had not decided to get in touch. There had been no upsurge of finer feelings. As if! she thought bitingly. His presence was sheer coincidence—a coincidence orchestrated by a peculiarly mischievous twist of fate.

'I'm helping Edith to run the Forgotten Eden,' she replied, and was surprised when the words emerged more or less normally.

With her mouth gone dry and her nerves giving a fair imitation of jangling piano wires, she had expected a puerile croak. But she had, she recalled, managed to play it cool to wondrous effect on one memorable occasion in the past, and apparently the knack had not deserted her.

'You work here?' Gifford said sharply.

She nodded. 'As general dogsbody. For example, this morning the cleaner has a dental appointment so I've been cleaning.'

His eyes trailed from the top of her tousled head, over her sweat-dampened top and creased shorts, and down the length of her legs to her thonged feet. When he had known her before she had worn smart, city-slicker suits and high heels, and had had her pale hair swept back in a smooth chignon. She had been elegance with a capital E. The only time she had looked tumbled was when they had been in bed. But she looked evocatively tumbled now. He frowned, remembering how good their lovemaking had been. How good they had been together in so many ways.

'So I see,' he muttered, making Cass feel even more conscious of her rumpled appearance. 'And Edith is—who?'

'She was my uncle Oscar's girlfriend. He died three months ago. Of cancer.'

Gifford lowered thick straight, dark brows. 'This is your uncle's place?' he queried. 'I remember you telling me how he owned a guest house and restaurant on Praslin—you spent holidays there—but I thought he'd sold it last year.'

'Oscar thought so, too, but at the very last minute the sale fell through and it's taken until now for another buyer to appear.' Cass hesitated, frowning. 'Though the deal's still to be finalised. Edith is a lovely lady, but not too worldly-wise,' she continued. 'When my uncle visited London last winter, he'd realised his days were numbered. He knew Edith would be out of her depth when it came to handling a sale, so he asked if I'd be willing to keep a long-distance eye on things.'

'Because he was aware that you are super-efficient?'

'Because I'm the only member of our family who's the least bit organised,' she countered, wondering if his comment should be interpreted as sarcastic. After all, she had been anything but efficient eighteen months ago.

'I was happy to agree,' she went on. 'But Edith took my agreement to mean hands-on help, and when the second purchaser surfaced she phoned to ask if I'd fly out. She was desperate for some support, and a change of scene suited me, so—'

Cass broke off. She was talking too much; it was an unfortunate tendency whenever she felt flustered. But there was no need to give him chapter and verse. Nor was there any reason to feel flustered. He was the villain

of the piece and the one who should be weighted down
with embarrassment, not her.

'So you're taking a sabbatical?' Gifford said.

'I suppose you could call it that. What about you? Are
you holidaying here or—' she offered up a silent prayer
'—have you come over from Mahé for the day?'

Although only seventeen miles long and, at its widest,
five miles across, Mahé was the largest of the one hun-
dred-plus islands of the Seychelles archipelago and the
home of the only town and capital, Victoria. Quiet and
unspoilt like all the islands, it boasted the most hotels,
the widest variety of watersports and the best choice of
boats.

A keen sportsman who thrived on action, Gifford
would want to sail, water-ski and snorkel. Yes, he would
be based there. Please. If she was to regain her equilib-
rium, she needed some distance between them—and a
distance filled by deep blue sea would surely help to
restrict his visits.

'I hate to dash your hopes,' he said curtly, 'but I'm
staying on Praslin.'

Her stomach churned. 'At Club Sesel?' she asked,
naming the only nearby hotel, which was a couple of
miles along the beach to the east and hidden behind a
headland.

She had, Cass realised, heard no sound of a car, and
for him to have arrived on foot it seemed he must have
come from there.

Gifford shook his head. 'No.'

'No?' she said, puzzled yet giving thanks for small
mercies. Almost all of the island's other hotels were sit-
uated on the opposite coast. True, they were only seven
or eight miles away, but it was better than nothing.

'I'm not booked into a hotel, I'm renting a house. I
arrived yesterday evening.'

'A house? Where?' she demanded.

He jerked a thumb. 'Thataway.'

Her thoughts hurtled in the same westerly direction, travelling around a small deep-water cove and up to a sprawling white bungalow which was surrounded by tall, flamboyant trees and bushes of pink and purple bougainvillea. Luxuriously furnished, the bungalow came with a wide rear terrace which provided panoramic views of the sea, and had a barbecue pit and a small indoor gym. It ranked five stars in the rental market.

'Maison d'Horizon?' Cass asked, and this time she did croak.

He gave a terse nod. 'I decided to spoil myself rotten.'

She glanced out of the restaurant to the wooden cottage where she was installed. 'But—but that makes you my neighbour!'

'Yup,' he said crustily. 'I'm the boy next door.'

Cass swallowed. Gifford Tait was not a boy, he was a man. A mature, experienced male who had done some serious damage to her heart, then strolled away and stayed away, leaving her to deal with the consequences.

'How long are you here for?' she enquired.

'Two months. Don't blame me,' he said, when she looked at him, appalled. 'It's your fault that I decided to come to the Seychelles.'

'My fault?' Cass protested.

'I remembered you saying how life here was peaceful and relaxed, and—' stretching out long fingers, he realigned the position of the white ceramic pepper pot '—I'm in need of relaxation.' His gaze swung to the vivid blue sea, along the arc of silvery coral sand, to green, shiny-leafed palm trees which were stirred by the balmy breeze. 'You also waxed lyrical about the beauty of the islands, and you didn't exaggerate.'

So coincidence was not responsible for this visitation;

the culprit had been her and her big mouth! And now they were destined to live with only a metaphorical garden fence between them. Her insides hollowed. It was much too close for comfort.

'The fourteen-hour days finally caught up on you?' she enquired, thinking that, as he played hard, so he worked hard, too.

'No, though I was overdoing it. For years I've been far too work-orientated.' Gifford poked at the pepper pot again. 'I've been…unwell, so I'm here to convalesce,' he said, and paused, plainly unwilling to go into detail. 'You couldn't find me something to eat in addition to coffee?'

Cass blinked. 'Excuse me?'

All the time they had been speaking, a thought had been hammering at the back of her mind—when would Gifford mention the baby? He might have ignored his existence this far, but he could not ignore it now. Yet she was damned if she would make things easier for him by referring to their son first.

'The rental agency was supposed to lay on a box of start-up groceries, but they've forgotten. They're sending one later, but I had nothing to eat last night and I'm starving.'

'Edith does the cooking, and she's out,' Cass said flatly.

His brows had lifted in an upward slant of appeal, but she refused to respond. She was no longer the adoring escort who rushed to obey his every request. The days of being charmed stupid were over. And if he fainted dead away from hunger, tough!

'It doesn't have to be something cooked. Bread and butter will do. Or fruit. You must have some fruit? If there's a packet of stale Cheezy Doodles or whatever lying around, I'll take that,' Gifford declared, with an air of stark desperation.

She shook her head. 'Sorry.'

'After travelling for damn near two days and crossing half the globe, I'm in no mood to be given the run-around,' he rasped, his grey eyes glittering. 'We both know the larder can't be completely bare, so—'

'How about scrambled eggs?' Cass suggested stiffly.

Being too uncooperative was not a smart move. Like it or not, there could be times in the future when she might need his goodwill, so she must bank down her hostility and keep things civil between them. It would not be easy, but...

'Scrambled eggs sounds great.' He flicked her a dry look. 'You aren't planning to poison me?'

'And risk the health authorities closing down the restaurant?' Her smile was razor-thin. 'Not worth it.'

'You've forgotten something,' Gifford said as she swung away.

She stopped and turned back. 'What?'

'You greeted me with "Good morning, sir" and now it should be "Not worth it, *sir*".' A dark brow rose a fraction. 'You must've heard of establishing good cus-tomer relations—or don't you aim to win the employee of the month award?'

'I'm not an employee, I'm a volunteer,' Cass told him crisply.

'Whatever your status, I am a customer,' he re-sponded. 'Which entitles me to a little...courtesy.'

Her full mouth thinned. He was deliberately baiting her. Once she would have found his sardonic humour amusing, but not now. Now she felt tempted to tell him to go take a long walk off a short pier—or something far coarser—but instead she slitted her eyes at him.

'In your dreams,' she said.

His lips twitched. He had always liked her verve and had enjoyed the cut-and-thrust repartee which they had often shared.

'Sassy as ever, I see.'

'You better believe it,' she responded, and stalked away.

In the kitchen, Cass swung into action, collecting eggs from the fridge, locating a pan, setting a tray. She had always imagined that when they did meet again—at her bidding, and at her choice of location—Gifford Tait would leave her cold, she reflected as she worked. Stone-cold. Alas, it was not so. With his thickly lashed grey eyes, features which were a touch too strong to be described as handsome, and lean, muscular physique, he continued to be disruptively—and alarmingly—virile. He also had undeniable charisma.

Reaching for a whisk, she beat the eggs fiercely. Snap out of it, she ordered herself. The dynamic Mr Tait may possess more than his fair share of sex appeal, but when it comes to caring and sharing and common-or-garden decency he rates a whopping great *minus*. Any charisma is superficial.

Gifford had been unwell. What did that mean? she wondered. She shrugged. He had not wanted to tell her and she would not ask.

The eggs were scrambled, sprinkled with chopped herbs, and arranged on a plate with triangles of hot, buttered toast. Lifting the tray, Cass steered out through the saloon-style swing doors which separated the kitchen from the restaurant. When she drew near, she saw that her customer was tapping the pepper pot up and down on the table in a sombre distracted rhythm. He looked uncharacteristically tense, like a man with a lot on his mind. As well he might, she thought astringently.

At the pad of her rubber-soled thongs on the plank floor, he glanced round.

'Quick service,' he said, as though she had caught him unawares in his introspection and caught him out.

'You'll be writing a letter of commendation to the Tourist Board?' she enquired.

'And faxing copies to the Prime Minister and President of the Seychelles,' he assured her, deadpan. As she served his food, a slow grin angled its way across his mouth. 'Do you finish off by bobbing a curtsy?'

'Don't push it,' Cass warned. 'You may be getting a kick out of this, but I have my limits.'

'A generous tip won't persuade you to curtsy?'

'I wouldn't curtsy if you sank to your knees, clasped your hands together and begged.' She tilted her head. 'Or perhaps I might. Going to try it?'

'Not my style,' Gifford replied.

'I thought not.'

He noticed that she had put down two cups and saucers. 'You're joining me?'

She nodded. They had to talk about the baby.

'I'm ready for a break,' she declared, thinking that what she really needed was a lie-down in a darkened room with cold compresses on her eyes and complete silence. 'You don't mind?' she asked, a touch belligerently.

'Be my guest,' he said, and, lifting his knife and fork, he began to eat.

As Cass poured the rich, dark, steaming coffee, she studied him from beneath her lashes. She had not noticed it when she had been looking down, but sitting directly across from him she saw that his face was leaner than she remembered and his high cheekbones were more sharply defined.

He had lost weight. Gifford also looked drawn—

which could be due to jet-lag, or to the shock of being confronted by her and the knowledge that he must soon meet the child whom they had both created.

'The restaurant may not open until noon, but everything seems remarkably organised,' he said, indicating the surrounding tables which were neatly set with gleaming cutlery and sparkling glasses.

'I was awoken at the crack of dawn, so I was able to get a good start,' Cass explained, and waited for him to ask about *who* had woken her up so early.

'Monday is a busy day?'

'Er—no. The busy days are Tuesdays, Thursdays and Saturdays, when we provide a buffet lunch for tour parties of around twenty or so. The rest of the time, it's quiet. The road outside is unmade and full of potholes—'

'I noticed when I was in the taxi,' he cut in, frowning, and briefly placed a hand on his thigh.

'And the prospect of such a bumpy ride puts people off. We get a few holidaymakers wandering down from Club Sesel, and the occasional determined backpacker, but it's the tour lunches which keep the place ticking over.'

'What do the tours take in?'

'They start off with a nature trail through the Vallée de Mai, which is an eerie and rather forbidding place, thick with palms, in the heart of Praslin. It's a World Heritage site. Next they come here for lunch, and then they drive up to Anse Lazio, a beach on the northern tip of the island which is great for swimming and snorkelling. You should go there some time.'

'Maybe,' Gifford said, frowning. He ate a few more mouthfuls. 'Your uncle was happy for things to just tick over?'

'Yes. Oscar was an ex-hippy who just wanted enough

to get by on, and to "hang loose".' Cass smiled, thinking fondly of her pony-tailed and somewhat eccentric uncle. A member of the peace-and-love brigade, he had been so laid-back as to be almost falling over. 'There's no word for "stress" in the Creole dictionary, so when he decided to live here he came to the perfect spot.'

'What about paying guests?' he asked.

'Oscar rarely advertised or did much in the way of repairs, so unfortunately those who managed to find their way here were not inclined to come again. The food is good—Edith's an excellent cook—but the accommodation's in urgent need of updating.'

'What is the accommodation?' Gifford enquired.

'Just the cottages,' she said, gesturing across the restaurant and out over an oval lawn of thick-bladed grass to where three pale blue wooden cottages sat in the dappled shade of stately palm trees. Tricked out with pointed arches and gingerbread eaves, they possessed a shabby, fairy-tale charm.

Gifford turned to look. 'No one's in residence?'

'I'm in the nearest one, but the others have been unoccupied since I arrived, and there are no forward bookings. Edith lives in the main house here, in a flat above the kitchen,' she added.

He set down his knife and fork. The plate was clean.

'That was ambrosia,' he told her.

'Thanks.'

'Thank you. I feel a darn sight more human now,' he said, and, easing back his chair and splaying his legs, he stretched lazily.

As he raised his arms, his shirt pulled up to reveal a strip of firm, flat midriff above the waistband of his jeans. Cass felt her heart start to pound. Her erstwhile lover was human; he was six feet three inches of powerfully constructed male. She could remember running her fingers over the hairy roughness of his chest, across that smooth midriff and down. She could remember the burn of his skin and—

'Are you here on your own?' he enquired.

She flushed. She had, she realised, been staring. Had Gifford noticed her fascination? Probably. He did not miss much.

She took a sip of coffee. Was she here alone? At long last, he had worked around to Jack. Alleluia! But what did he think she had done? Parked the baby with someone and swanned off unencumbered to the tropical sunshine? Come *on*! Yet by avoiding a direct question Gifford was playing games. She shot him an impatient glance. OK, she would play games, too.

'On my own?' Cass repeated, all innocence.

'There's no man around?'

She opened her blue eyes wide. If he wanted to be obtuse, she would also be obtuse.

'Man?' she enquired.

'Is Stephen with you?' he said, and heard the curtness of his voice reflect his distaste for the idea.

'Stephen?' She gave a startled laugh. 'No.'

Stephen was Stephen Dexter, head of the Dexter sports equipment company which had been bought out the previous year by the vigorously expanding Tait-Hill Corporation. She had worked for the young man, first as his secretary, then as his personal assistant, and later in the upgraded role of business aide.

'Does Edith do all the cooking or do you lend a hand there, too?' Gifford asked.

Cass looked blank. She had been thinking how Stephen had been a loyal and generous friend, but hopeless when it came to trade. It had been his incompetence which had hastened the family firm's decline, made it ripe for a take-over and thus brought Gifford Tait into her life.

'I help with minor tasks sometimes—like peeling vegetables—but Edith plans the menus and makes all the dishes. I wonder what's happened to her?' she carried on, inspecting the slim gold watch which encircled her wrist. 'She's gone to visit her sister and taken—'

Cass bit off the words. She had been on the brink of saying that Edith had taken Jack along in his buggy to be fussed over and admired—all the Seychellois seemed to love children—but she refused to open up the subject. The lengthy months of silence had made it clear that Gifford regarded her pregnancy as her fault and the baby as her responsibility—a responsibility which she had willingly accepted. But it was now a point of principle that *he* must refer to their son first.

'Edith should be back at any moment,' she said.

He drank a mouthful of coffee. 'Whoever's buying this place must believe they can drum up customers from somewhere,' he remarked.

She balled her fists, the knuckles draining white. He was a perverse so-and-so. His refusal to speak of Jack—innocent, adorable, fatherless Jack—made her want to throw things at him. Hard. In the past, Gifford had exhibited a straight-arrow approach to problems—an approach which could be ruthless, as she knew to her cost—so why was he avoiding this issue now?

Cass shot him a look from beneath her too long fringe. Could he be embarrassed by his failure to respond to her letters, make contact and offer help? He was far too urbane an individual to visibly squirm, but did he feel ashamed? Might he want to say sorry, yet be tongue-tied by thoughts of his abysmal behaviour?

'Apparently,' she said, thinking that when he did

pluck up the courage to apologise she would take immense satisfaction in watching him grovel.

'Has the guy run a hotel before?'

'Yes, in South Africa.'

'What made him decide to come here?'

'I've no idea,' Cass said impatiently. Once upon a time they had spent hours avidly discussing business matters, but the pressing topic for discussion now was Jack. Her darling Jack. 'Edith had the first dealings, and although I met him when he called in a couple of weeks ago basically all I know is that his name is Kirk Weber and he comes from Johannesburg.'

'What's he like?' Gifford asked.

'In his forties, good-looking, friendly. Edith thinks he's the bee's knees and calls him Mr Wonderful.'

'You said he's yet to close the sale.'

She nodded. 'It was supposed to go through a month ago, but Kirk's been having difficulty transferring his funds, and since then—zilch.'

'Perhaps he's changed his mind.'

Her brow crinkled. 'I don't think so. He insists the money is on its way and rings every few days to check that no one else has been to look at the property.'

'Edith always tells him no?'

'Yes.'

'An error.'

'Could be,' Cass acknowledged.

'*Is*. Damn.'

As Gifford had spoken, he had slashed out a hand in emphasis and knocked a spare knife from the table, sending it flying and clattering to the floor a couple of yards away.

She waited for him to rise and, with the athletic grace which she remembered so well, retrieve the knife, but when he didn't she pushed back her chair. Collecting fallen cutlery had, it seemed, been designated as the waitress's work. Cass bent, picked up the knife and polished it on a napkin.

She thrust it towards him. 'May I return this?' she said.

'You're too kind.'

'It's all part of the service.'

Amusement quirked in one corner of his mouth. 'And you've resisted the urge to carve me up into little pieces.'

She shone a saccharine smile at him. 'Just.'

As she handed him the knife, their fingers touched. Cass stood rigid. The brush of his skin against hers seemed to create an electric current which tingled in her fingertips and shot up her arm.

'You look…different,' Gifford said, his grey eyes starting to move over her in a slow inspection.

Once again, she drew in her stomach. Since arriving on the island a month ago she had exercised every day, and soon she would be firm and trim—back to her original figure. But right now her belly remained a touch flabby.

'I've put on weight which I'm trying to shed. Though it's hardly surprising. Is it?' she challenged.

'You mean because you're living alongside a restaurant, day in, day out?' He pursed his lips. 'I guess not.'

Cass glared. He was so infuriating, so frustrating. I mean because I've had a baby! she yelled inside her head.

'Your breasts are fuller,' he murmured, and lifted his gaze to hers.

Her heartbeat quickened. She still attracted him. She could see it in the smoky depths of his eyes and hear it in the sensual purr of his voice. She sank down onto her chair. Half of her was pleased, smug even—but the other half, the sensible half, insisted that, from now on, their relationship must be strictly neutral and strictly business. It had been the sexual draw which had caused so much havoc before, but she would not make the same mistake twice.

She was on the point of telling him that she did not appreciate such personal comments when she noticed that Gifford was frowning. He, too, seemed to regret his observation. And no doubt regretted that she still appealed, Cass thought drily.

'Me and Phyllis were so busy chattin' the time went flyin' by,' someone announced into the silence, and they both jumped and looked round.

A plumply handsome black woman had pushed out through the kitchen doors. Her lustrous dark hair was piled into a bun on the top of her head and she wore a floral button-through dress. She was in her mid-fifties.

'Hello, Edith,' Cass said, smiling, then she frowned. Where was Jack?

'His lordship's flat out on the verandah,' the new arrival advised, as if reading her mind. She nodded at Gifford. *'Bonzour.'*

'Good morning,' he replied.

'Cassie opened up early and made you something to eat? You must be special,' Edith declared, her brown eyes twinkling.

Cass gave a strained smile. Should she say that they knew each other? If so, how much did she reveal? She had told the older woman that Jack's father was not around, and as man/woman relationships in the Seychelles often seemed to be casual and temporary— *en passant* was the local term—her statement had been accepted without question. Gifford had not been named.

'This is Mr Tait,' she said. 'He's moved into Maison d'Horizon.'

Edith chuckled. 'You *are* special,' she declared, in her rolling, molasses-rich Creole-accented English. She turned to Cass. 'Have you asked if—'

'No, and I'm not going to,' she cut in hurriedly.

'Aw, honey, Bernard didn't mind, and I'm sure Mr Tait—'

'Please call me Gifford,' Gifford said, with a smile.

Edith smiled back. Some people you took an instant liking to, and Edith obviously liked him. 'I'm sure Gifford,' she adjusted, 'won't mind, either.'

'I mind,' Cass insisted, shooting the older woman a fiercely pleading 'keep quiet' look.

'Mind about what?' Gifford enquired.

'Us asking a couple of favours,' Edith told him. 'Bernard was the French gentleman who rented Maison d'Horizon before you. He was gettin' on, in his seventies, and came out here to take a break from his ever-naggin' wife and to make drawings of the birds—the parrots, mynahs and such. The island is full of them. He was so obliging.'

Cass gritted her teeth. She knew what was coming next.

'Look, I—' she started to protest, but the woman refused to be deflected.

'Bernard used to come in for meals and a drink at the bar most evenings, and when he heard how we've been waiting for a delivery of water glasses since kingdom come—' Edith rolled despairing eyes '—he brought over two dozen. Don't know who it was who stocked the villa, but they sure went to town on glasses. Went to town on most everything, like the exercise machines, as you'll have seen. Bernard never used the machines, but—'

'Gifford is a keep-fit fanatic and he will,' Cass inserted, at speed. 'Yes?'

His brow furrowed. 'Yes.'

'Even so,' Edith continued blithely, 'you're not going to be exercisin' all of the time. Cassie here's hung up on slimming down her figure, though Lord knows why because she looks more than slim enough to me. Real shapely.'

His eyes moved over Cass again. 'True,' he agreed, and his frown cut deeper.

'Bernard was happy for her to work out whenever she wished, so—'

'You want to borrow the glasses again, and Cass would like to make it burn?' Gifford enquired, in a slightly terse summing-up.

He had chosen the Seychelles for his recuperation be- . cause the islands were a very long way from home. He had wanted to be anonymous, living alone and keeping himself to himself, with no visitors. He had never imagined he would meet anyone he knew, least of all Cass.

The black woman grinned. 'Please.'

Frowning, he considered the proposition, then he nodded. 'Sure.'

'There you are,' Edith said, swinging Cass a triumphant smile. 'Must go now and start on lunch.' She reverted to her native Creole. *'Orevwar.'*

'Au revoir,' Gifford said.

'Edith was speaking out of turn,' Cass began as the swing doors dovetailed shut. 'We can manage without—'

'There's no need to manage. Give me a ring to let me know when you're coming and you can have the glasses,' he told her. 'We can also fix a time for your aerobics sessions.'

She dithered. His agreement had been reluctant and, call it foolish pride, but she did not want to be the re-

cipient of his largesse. Yet she was keen to lose those
few excess pounds.

'Thanks. Will do.'

'Fitting out the gym must've cost an obscene amount
of money,' Gifford remarked. 'Take the computerised
exercise bike. The only place I've ever seen a machine
like that before was in an exclusive sports club in Aspen.
It...'

As he talked on, Cass drank the rest of her coffee. He
had failed to make any mention of Jack. How could he?
She felt so hurt, so wounded, that he had not immediately demanded to see her—his—child. Didn't he care
about him just a little? Didn't he feel any curiosity? Or
compassion? The answer had to be a resounding *no*.

Her hurt hardened into a cold, stony anger and, clattering her cup down onto her saucer, she rose to her feet.
Gifford might resent being landed with a son, but she
would make him acknowledge and accept him.

'Back in a minute,' she said, and marched away.

Passing Edith, who was dicing sweet potato in the
kitchen, she went through the wedged-open side door
and out onto the verandah. There, in the shade, stood a
navy-upholstered baby buggy. Walking quietly over,
Cass looked down. With his thumb fallen from his
mouth and his dark lashes spread on peach-smooth
cheeks, Jack was fast asleep. She felt a catch in her
throat. She loved him so much.

Her forehead puckered. She had always known that
he looked like Gifford, but until she had seen them together—almost—she had not realised how strong the resemblance was. Their dark hair grew in the same way,
they had the same broad brow, the same determined
chin. But she would, she thought fiercely, do her
damnedest to ensure that Jack grew up with a far softer
heart.

Releasing the brake, she took a grip on the push-bar. Like it or not, the unwilling father was going to meet his son—*now*.

Cass wheeled the buggy through the kitchen and, holding one of the swing doors aside, strode forward. She stopped dead. The table was empty. A sheaf of notes in payment for his meal was tucked beneath a saucer, but Gifford had gone.

The prospect of coming face to face with his offspring must have been too much to take, so he had fled the restaurant. Was he also intending to flee from the bungalow and from the island? By the end of the day, would Gifford Tait be flying back to the States? She tossed her head. She could think of nothing which would suit her better.

CHAPTER TWO

THE hair stylist smiled down into the buggy. 'Doesn't your mama look as pretty as a princess?' she enquired.

The baby grinned, blue-grey eyes smiling and a dimple denting one round cheek, then he pursed his rosebud lips and blew a raspberry.

Cass laughed. 'He may not be too thrilled, but I think it's a big improvement.' She took a final, appraising look at herself in the mirror. 'Thanks a lot.'

Gifford's arrival the previous day had had one plus, she thought wryly as she steered the pushchair out of the salon and started off along the spacious marble-floored lobby of Club Sesel. The interruption had made her think twice about wielding the scissors.

Past experience had shown that she was a 'chop-aholic', so chances were her hair would have wound up looking as if it had been sheared by a lunatic with a chainsaw. Instead, her fringe was softly feathered, while the fall of burnished wheat-gold hair ended in a straight line at her shoulders. Cass tweaked at the silky black top which she wore with stone-coloured chinos. Today she looked stylish. Stylish enough to be mistaken for a hotel guest.

Club Sesel—Sesel was the Creole word for the Seychelles—catered for the wealthy. Guests stayed in individual granite bungalows which were discreetly sited amidst landscaped hillside gardens full of tropical blooms, ate in a chandeliered dining hall and could browse in the designer outlets which lined the lobby. She swung a look around. The lobby and shops were cur-

27

rently deserted. In general, there seemed to be few guests.

Reaching the gift shop, Cass stopped to study a window display which featured exclusive beachwear and mother-of-pearl jewellery arranged around a pair of polished coco de mer nuts. The huge nuts, which had a suggestively intimate female shape, were reputed to grow only in the Seychelles. These days restricted numbers were sold as expensive souvenirs, though in the past their kernels had been regularly ground up and used as an aphrodisiac.

A shadow clouded her blue eyes. There had been no need for aphrodisiacs when she and Gifford had met. Like their emotional rapport, the sexual attraction had been instant and compelling. And when they had made love it had been a passionate explosion of feeling which—

Her gaze swung sideways. A door bearing the word 'Manager' in gold letters had been opened, drawing her attention, but the man who had started to come out had swivelled and was disappearing inside again. As the door clicked shut behind him, Cass frowned. With well-groomed fair hair, and wearing a silver-grey gabardine suit, he had looked suspiciously like Kirk Weber. She did not know where the South African stayed when he came to the island—nor had she been aware that he was here now—but Club Sesel would be handy for him.

Setting off again, she negotiated the buggy down a couple of shallow steps and out into the dazzling sunshine of the paved forecourt. Could Kirk's presence mean he was about to finalise his purchase of the Forgotten Eden? she wondered as she slid on her dark glasses. She crossed mental fingers. She hoped so.

'Yoo-hoo, Cass!' a voice shrilled, and when she turned she saw a woman with short, gel-slicked auburn hair and wearing a gold lamé swimsuit waving at her from the far side of the small kidney-shaped swimming pool.

'Hello, Veronica,' she called back, smiling, and waited as the redhead teetered towards her on high gold-sandalled heels.

Over the past two weeks, Veronica Milne had become a regular visitor to the Forgotten Eden. She would arrive in her hire-car around midday or in the evening, pick at her meal, then switch to sit at the bar where she would make eyes at Jules Adonis, the Seychellois barman who, with clean-cut looks, long, sun-lightened dreadlocks and a beguiling white smile, lived up to his surname. A surname which was surprisingly common in the islands.

If the baby happened to be around, she also made a big fuss of him.

A thin, twittery woman who talked non-stop, Veronica was hard going after the first five minutes—but Cass felt sorry for her. Behind the determinedly bright expression, she sensed a lost soul.

'Just thought I'd tell you that I shall be along for lunch today,' Veronica said. 'Will Jules be there?'

'He should be, though he has been known to sleep in and not wake up until it's too late. Or forget which day it is,' she said ruefully.

'He's such a heartthrob. Like this little fellow,' the redhead declared, stretching down a hand to tickle the baby's tummy.

Jack wriggled and giggled.

'Do you have children?' Cass enquired.

Veronica straightened. 'No. I run my own fashion boutique—we sell only the best names—and there's never been time to fit in a family. And now I'm divorced; the decree absolute came through last month. This is the first time I've been on holiday on my own.

The first time I'll go back to an empty house.' She looked down at her noticeably denuded wedding-ring finger, though her other fingers were banded with rings of all shapes and sizes. 'Of course, I could always marry again and have a baby. I'm only just into my forties, so it isn't too late.'

'I suppose not,' Cass said, and hoped she did not sound doubtful.

'I think Jules fancies me,' Veronica declared, and lowered her voice into a giggly, conspiratorial whisper. 'I fancy him, too.'

Cass felt a stab of concern. The woman might sport a trendy elf-in-a-rainstorm hairstyle and wear glamorous clothes, but rather than 'just into' her forties she looked more in her mid-forties, if not heading towards fifty. Jules was twenty-five.

He was also a happy-go-lucky Romeo who flirted with females—any female—out of habit and on autopilot. She had assumed this was glaringly obvious, but perhaps Veronica preferred not to see? Newly divorced, she could be feeling adrift and eager for male attention. Too eager.

'Jules has a girlfriend,' Cass said gently, not wanting her to get hurt. 'In fact, he has several. I must go. I look forward to seeing you later. Goodbye.'

'Bye, bye,' Veronica trilled; but she was smiling at Jack and waving.

Cass pushed the buggy up the hotel's sloping drive and out onto the hard-baked red earth of the road. She had spent most of last night tossing and turning and thinking about Gifford, and as she set off for the Forgotten Eden her mind returned to him again.

Yesterday, her reaction to his exit from the restaurant had been, Good riddance! But it had been a knee-jerk reaction. And he had not fled the island. A distant glimmer of lights from the bungalow the previous evening, plus the slam of a door this morning, had indicated that he remained in residence.

She frowned. Whilst becoming a single parent had never featured in her scheme of things—heaven forbid!—she had coped with all the various traumas and got her life back on track. Plans had been made for the future. But now Gifford had appeared and thrown everything into confusion.

'I was going to send your daddy photographs of you on your first birthday,' she said, speaking to the baby who sat in the pushchair. 'And if he didn't reply I was going to send another batch when you reached two. Then, if that failed to produce a response, I intended to take you over to the States, plop you on the middle of his office desk and say, Hey, buster, I'd like to introduce your son and heir. That would've concentrated his mind, yes?'

Jack clapped small, starfished hands—his latest trick.

'I don't expect him to be an every-day daddy,' Cass continued, becoming grave, 'but I believe that every child has the right to know its father, and I want him to show a respectable amount of care and consideration. Like remembering your birthdays and taking you on the occasional holiday when you're a big boy, and being available at times when you particularly need a dad.'

'Blah,' her listener said.

'I was going to tell him all this when you were two. When you'd be starting to realise that other children have daddies and wondering where yours had got to. Only he's turned up now.'

The baby stuck his thumb in his mouth and sucked noisily.

There could, of course, be a second reason for Gifford's abrupt departure from the restaurant, Cass reflected. He might have been eager to return to a companion. A female companion, whom he had left in bed. He was a red-blooded male with all the usual appetites—as she could confirm, she thought astringently—and whilst he might be here to convalesce she could not imagine him spending the days alone and doing nothing. So it seemed possible that he had a woman in tow.

Halting, she lowered the buggy into its recline position, laid down her son and drew forward the hood. Jack's chubby arms and legs were lightly tanned, but she was wary of him getting too much sun.

Cass walked on. Might Gifford's companion be the glamorous Imogen Sales? The more she thought about his attitude the previous day, the more she felt there had been an air of strained secrecy about him. He had been hiding something. What? The fact that he had come to the Seychelles with the actress who had followed her into his arms and his affections with insulting, hurtful speed?

She pushed the buggy down into a crater of a pothole and up out of it again. A few months ago she had seen the American woman in a TV film. Cass grimaced. She had had the kind of shiny, swinging raven-black bob which was more usually seen in shampoo adverts, a serenely aloof face and, wearing a succession of slinky numbers, had been disgustingly slim. Imogen had also, she thought cattily, displayed an inescapable need to pose and possessed all the acting skills of cardboard.

Her expression shadowed. She did not welcome the idea of producing Jack and discussing what were essentially private matters with Imogen Sales around. Yet, even if the actress or some other woman was living with Gifford in the villa, it was vital that they should talk. For her son's sake, lines of communication needed to be established.

Cass strode on. Once upon a time, she had considered herself to be a good judge of character. She had been convinced that her lover was conscientious, reliable, trustworthy, but it had been all smoke and mirrors.

'How could I have been so wrong?' she muttered, and fell silent, bombarded with memories of the past...

It had been Henry Dexter, Stephen's elderly father and, at that time, head of the company, who had first brought the Tait-Hill Corporation to her attention.

'Those two will go far,' he had declared, marching into his son's office one morning to thrust a trade magazine at him. 'Read the article and see how ambitious they are, how well informed and on the ball.' He had frowned. 'Take note of how hard they work.'

'Yes, Pa,' Stephen had replied obediently, but he had put the magazine aside and not bothered.

Cass had read the article; as a new and keen secretary she'd read all the memos and reports which the young man was supposed to read but often did not. It had told how two Americans, Gifford Tait and Bruce Hill, had once been skiers representing their country at world-class level and winning medals. Both business graduates, they had seen a need in their sport for better-designed equipment and decided to satisfy it.

Over the next few years, the old man's prophecy had come true. Tait-Hill had flourished, widening their product range to other sports and developing an eclectic spread of business interests which included property, a hot-air-balloon company and a million-dollar stake in a computer software manufacturer.

However, after Henry suffered a stroke and was forced to retire, Dexter's had gone downhill. A traditional, slightly old-fashioned firm whose name on cricket bats, tennis rackets and running shoes guaranteed top quality, its future had begun to look shaky. Then a letter had been received from Tait-Hill, suggesting talks about a rescue package and possible buy-out.

Despite Stephen's claim that he could turn things around—and much to his chagrin—his father had decreed that Tait-Hill must be allowed to vet the company for potential acquisition. A short while later, Gifford had flown in.

After a week spent poring over balance sheets at the London headquarters and assessing financial information—information which Cass had invariably provided—he had requested that she give him a crash course on the workings of Dexter's and provide details of the company's forward plans.

'Why me?' she asked, thinking of how she had left Stephen sulking in his office.

'Because you're the smart kid around here.' Gifford grinned at her across the desk. 'And because I like you.'

She laughed. From the start they had worked well together, and had soon discovered that they shared the same sense of humour.

'I quite like you, too,' she said.

'Only quite?' he protested, with mock anguish. 'I must switch my manly charm up a gear.'

'You have charm?' Cass enquired, straight-faced.

'You never noticed?'

'Maybe just a flicker, now and then.'

'Which means I'm starting virtually from scratch.' Gifford gave a noisy sigh. 'So be it.'

In the days which they spent closeted together, Cass grew to like Gifford Tait a lot. He knew what he wanted and could be autocratic, but he was also modest, funny and easy to be with. He exuded an inherent vitality which dimmed the memory of every other man she had known. Plus he was indecently sexy.

When, unexpectedly, he had to fly back to the States to deal with an urgent business matter, she had felt confusingly bereft and had spent every spare moment thinking about him.

'Did you miss me?' Gifford enquired, on his return a week or so later.

'Yes,' she said truthfully.

'I missed you, too,' he told her, his grey eyes serious. 'I figure I need to spend a month getting to grips with Dexter's, so—'

'That long?' she interrupted.

He gave a crooked grin. 'That long. So I wondered whether you'd be free to show me around London at the weekends.'

'With pleasure,' Cass said.

They visited museums and art galleries, watched the street performers at Covent Garden, went to the theatre. They sailed down the river to Greenwich and the gleaming silver stanchions of the Thames Barrier, and shared candlelit dinners.

Their relationship deepened. Away from the office, Gifford would reach for her hand, and when he returned her to her Putney flat in the evenings he kissed her goodnight. They were passionate kisses which left her weak-kneed and breathless—and wanting more.

Time flew and, all too soon, they reached the final week of his stay when they set off on a fact-finding tour of the Dexter factories.

'How did you first start up in your business?' Cass asked curiously one evening when they were sitting in his hotel suite.

They had spent the wet, blustery April day at a shoe-manufacturing unit in the north of England. On their return, she had typed out the notes which her companion had required on her laptop, and now they were unwinding with a bottle of good white wine.

'Thanks to dumb luck,' Gifford replied. 'Bruce and I were bursting with ideas, but we didn't have either the cash or the know-how to put them into action. Then a ski-wear manufacturer happened to catch me on TV.'

'When you were skiing?'

'Commentating.'

She looked at him along the sofa. 'You commentate?' she said, in surprise.

'Used to. At one point, I fronted a sports programme.' He raked back the cow-lick of dark hair which persisted in falling over his eyes. 'But I quit.'

'Why?'

'Didn't care for the fame. The show was aired in several states which meant I was becoming a celebrity, but I don't like being pounced on by strangers or having journalists pry into my private life. The ski-wear manufacturer asked if I'd promote his products,' Gifford continued. 'At which point Bruce and I hit him with our brainwaves. He gave us a loan, factory space and—' he clicked his fingers '—abracadabra.'

'It can't have been that simple,' Cass protested.

'It wasn't,' he admitted, with a rueful smile. 'As new kids on the block it took a hell of a lot of blood, sweat and tears—of lugging samples around and cold calling— before we were up and rolling, but now—'

'Life is good?'

Reaching out a hand, he tucked a strand of silky wheat-gold hair behind her ear. 'Right now, life is very good,' he said softly.

Her heart began to thud. The anonymous hotel suite, the rain which pattered on the windows, the leaden evening sky—everything faded. Her only awareness was of Gifford—his touch, the husky timbre of his voice, the need which she saw in his grey eyes. A need which she suspected was reflected in her own.

He sat back, loosening his tie in what struck her as an attractively masculine gesture. 'Your boss isn't into blood, sweat and tears,' he said. 'He might get a kick out of being the big cheese and having his name painted on the best parking space, but he resents having to come into the office day after day.'

Cass hesitated. A sense of loyalty tempted her to insist otherwise—and lie through her teeth. But Gifford would know she was lying.

'From his birth it was decreed that Stephen would take over from his father. It's the family tradition,' she explained, 'but he lacks any real interest.'

'Whereas you are interested. You know what's happening in all areas of the business, and you have savvy, which is why I asked for you to accompany me.'

'Asked?' Cass said. 'It sounded more like a demand.'

A grin cut across his mouth. 'OK, I demanded. But if Stephen'd come along he'd have been worse than useless. You're carrying the guy. I hope he's paying you a high salary?'

'So high I'd be foolish to ever leave,' she replied.

'What goes on between you two?' Gifford enquired as he sipped his wine. He fixed her with narrowed grey eyes. 'You're obviously close, and Stephen gave me the impression that—'

'That what?' Cass asked, when he frowned.

'That you might have a…more personal involvement.'

She burst out laughing. 'Stephen and me? No, you must've misunderstood. I've worked for him for a long time, but although he's a couple of years older than me Stephen's like a kid brother.'

'A self-centred and petulant kid brother,' Gifford said. He knew he was not mistaken and that the younger man had deliberately given him the wrong impression. Maybe to warn him off?

'On occasions,' she had to agree. 'But he can also be kind, thoughtful and fun. His father dominates him, while his mother has always spoiled him—Stephen was a late baby and an only child—and that's a difficult mix for anyone to handle.'

'Parents can land their kids with all kinds of problems,' he said gravely, and was silent for a moment. Then he gave a satisfied nod. 'You and Stephen are just friends—good.'

'Why good?'

'Because it means you don't have a serious man in your life, so—'

'What makes you sure of that?' Cass interrupted.

'You haven't phoned anyone while we've been on our travels or spoken about anyone.' He shot her a suddenly worried look. 'I don't doubt you have to beat the guys off with a stick, but is there anyone serious?'

She shook her head. Although she was twenty-seven, she had only had one serious relationship, but that had run out of steam over a year ago.

'Not at the moment.'

'Thank God. So you won't have any hang-ups about us making love,' Gifford completed.

All of a sudden, the air seemed to throb.

'Making love?' she repeated, with care.

'It's inevitable.'

'You think so?'

'I do.' Moving closer, Gifford took the glass which she held in increasingly shaky fingers and set it aside with his on a low table. 'And it's another reason—probably the main reason—why I demanded that you accompany me.'

'You are sly and underhand,' Cass informed him. 'A self-serving shark.'

'Aren't I just?' he said, and smiled a smile so ravishing it could have melted a stone. It melted her heart. 'But you think that us making love is inevitable, too.' Framing her face with his hands, he looked deep into her eyes. 'You know that sooner or later we're going to wind up in bed. Yes?'

She gulped in a breath. Why deny the truth?

'Yes.'

'You want me and I want you. I want you so much it's all I can think about. You're driving me crazy.' He raised anguished brows. 'Hell, Cass, I'm suffering here.'

She grinned. 'You'd like me to take pity and put you out of your misery?'

'It'd be a humane gesture of the greatest magnanimity. Now…' he said, and he drew her close and kissed her.

His lips parted her lips. The muscle of his tongue explored the velvet confines of her mouth, and utterly seduced her. With her hands clutching at his shoulders, her head spinning and her senses reeling, Cass flowed into the kiss. She needed him. For so long, she had ached for him. As she wrapped herself closer around him, they kissed again. Their breathing quickened, then Gifford was leading her through to his bedroom and swiftly undressing her.

'You're beautiful, Cass,' he said, when she stood naked before him. His eyes roamed over her high breasts with their taut nipples, down across the smooth plane of her belly to the fair curls which grew at the crevice of her thighs. He raised his head, and, reaching out a hand, withdrew the tortoiseshell comb which secured her hair. 'Beautiful,' he repeated huskily as the heavy strands swirled down to rest on her shoulders in a gleaming wheaten curtain.

Cass stepped closer, her fingers going to the buttons on his shirt. 'My turn,' she said, a little breathlessly, and he smiled.

'Your turn,' Gifford agreed, and helped her.

Naked and entwined together on the bed, they kissed again. As they kissed, Gifford began to touch her, his thumbs brushing across the rigidity of her nipples, his fingers caressing the swollen globes of her breasts. She stirred restlessly in his arms.

'Please,' she said. 'Please.'

He was a sensitive lover, tender and yet sure. As in business matters, he knew what he wanted. He took— and gave. When he entered her, Cass thought she might die from the spiralling emotion. But he was urging her on, and on. A throaty moan told of her passion. She had not felt such raw desire before nor experienced such primitive need...and had never known such an overwhelming relief.

The remainder of their tour fused into one glorious blur of lovemaking, though other factories were visited, facts gleaned and reports typed. On their return to London, an awareness of time fast running out made the days more precious, the intimacy more urgent. In three days, then two, then one, Gifford was due to fly back to Boston.

'We should talk,' he declared as they finished breakfast on the morning of his departure.

He had cancelled the classy hotel room which she had booked for him and joined her in her far more humble Putney flat. They had awoken in the early hours and made love with sweet desperation, then, when the alarm had rung, dragged themselves out of bed and gone for a run. At home he ran several miles every morning, he'd told her.

Coming back, Gifford had headed for the shower,

while she'd prepared toast and coffee. When Cass had walked through and seen the water sluicing down the hard planes of his naked body, she had impetuously flung off her clothes and joined him beneath the spray. Passion had claimed them again.

'Talk about what?' she enquired now.

'About us,' he said soberly.

Her heart performed a long, slow somersault. It might be madness, but she wondered if he was going to propose. Granted, they had only known each other for a couple of months at most, yet she knew that she loved him. She suspected that Gifford had fallen in love with her, too. The word had not been spoken and no promises had been made, but they seemed so right together. They enjoyed a natural rapport, and the sexual alchemy was magic. They were kindred spirits.

'What about us?' Cass asked, and was unable to keep from smiling.

He was the man she had been hoping for, waiting to love, all her life. The sheer joy of being with him, combined with the sense of absolute comfort which she felt in his presence, insisted that this was the real thing.

'Our affair's been...hot, but I figure we should cool it,' Gifford said, and moistened his lips. Although he had rehearsed his speech it was not coming easily, but a panicky feeling of self-preservation insisted that it must be said. 'As you know, I'll be recommending to Bruce that we buy Dexter's, so chances are we shall meet in the future,' he continued. 'But, whilst it may be a cliché, mixing business with pleasure does complicate matters and isn't such a clever idea.'

Cass's heart crash-landed, but her smile remained sturdily in place. His words had stabbed like small, sharp daggers ripping into her flesh. She had not been having an 'affair'; she had been involved in a romance. A romance which she had believed was destined to grow into a close relationship, mature and lasting.

'I agree,'she said.

Pushing up from his chair, Gifford jammed his fists into his trouser pockets and started to pace around the small kitchen. 'Getting serious wouldn't be such a clever idea, either. I have to be honest and admit that I have this dread of being tied down. I'm not cut out for domesticity. I like to be independent, free to go where I want, when I want. I like to be able to ski or sail, or go away on business with no—' All of a sudden, he broke off and turned to face her. 'You agree?' he said, as though her words had only just penetrated.

'I do. And I never imagined for one moment that we might get serious.'

His brows came down. 'You didn't?'

'Good grief, *no*! Our affair's been fun—' she released a merry chortle of laughter '—but it wasn't of the lasting variety. As for domesticity, I'm not ready to settle down, either. Not yet. Not for a long time.'

Gifford raked a hand back through the thickness of his dark hair. He looked surprised, yet relieved. Had he expected her to argue or hurl furious recriminations or perhaps burst into floods of tears? she wondered. Her backbone stiffened. It was the first time a man had given her the brush-off, but she was damned if she would cry.

'You said you'd ring for a cab to take me to the airport,' he reminded her.

'Right away,' she said brightly. 'Right away.'

What a fool she had been, Cass thought, after he had gone. What a slow-witted, unaware fool. Gifford Tait was such a desirable package—striking looks, athletic physique, healthy bank balance—that legions of women would have hurled themselves at him. Yet for thirty-six years he had remained single. So it followed that he must be actively opposed to commitment. He had never thought in terms of loving her. As for them being kindred spirits—it had been a rosy illusion.

As if to provide proof, a month later she came across a photograph of him at the launch of a TV sports station in a US trade journal. He was standing with Imogen Sales draped around him like a clinging ivy and, in the write-up, the actress, who also came from Boston, was quoted as coyly admitting that they were 'an item'.

Cass had dropped the journal into the waste-paper basket. She'd refused to collapse in a heap or to bellyache. Gifford Tait would be regarded as a 'step up the learning curve'—albeit one of the harsher kind—and dismissed from her mind. Given enough time.

But a couple of weeks later the doctor confirmed her suspicion that she was pregnant…

By the time she turned into the drive which led haphazardly down through lacy casuarina trees to the Forgotten Eden, Jack was fast asleep. Cass parked the buggy on the verandah beside the wedged-open kitchen door and went inside.

Edith was in the midst of preparing lunch while Marquise, the chatty teenaged cleaner and part-time waitress, filled vases with sprigs of hibiscus.

'I like your hair,' Edith said.

'Looks real classy,' Marquise piped up.

Cass grinned. 'Thanks. What can I do?'

'You can go next door and get those water glasses,' Edith said, deftly filleting the freshly caught kingfish which would be baked with garlic and served in a tangy lemon sauce. 'And while you're there you can hop on that exercise bike.'

'The tour group'll be arriving soon,' Cass demurred. She knew she must confront Gifford—and for her to choose the time and place would be preferable to him coming into the restaurant again and surprising her—yet she was not sure she felt ready to confront him right now.

'The tour group won't be here for another hour, which gives you plenty of time. And they're the reason why we could do with the glasses. Marquise and I'll keep an eye out for *bébé* waking up.' Edith shooed her off with a wave of her hand. 'Now go!'

Once in her cottage, Cass changed into a lavender-coloured leotard, pulled on a pair of grey knit shorts and tied the laces on her trainers. She would, she decided, start by saying that their son was, naturally, with her, and suggest that Gifford might like to see him. Her demeanour would be cool, calm and uncritical. Whilst she longed to deliver a volley of vitriolic home truths and savagely denounce him, for Jack's sake she could not afford to turn him into an enemy.

The Forgotten Eden sat on a tongue of lush land which ended in a strip of white coral sand at the Indian Ocean. To the east stretched a long, shallow bay, while to the west was the tight horseshoe of the granite boulder-edged cove. Taking a path which skirted the cove and cut up through the trees, Cass set off towards Maison d'Horizon.

Sunlight dappled the yellow-green fronds of palms and lit strands of purple orchids which hung from the trees. There were glimpses of sun-sparkled sea. Dragonflies whizzed around like miniature coloured helicopters.

According to a guide book she had read, when General Charles Gordon, the hero of Khartoum, had visited Praslin in the late 1800s he'd believed he had found the biblical Garden of Eden. She smiled. She could understand his belief.

With thickly wooded hills strewn with huge, cathedral-grand boulders and a wealth of wild blossoms, Praslin had to be one of the most beautiful islands on earth. It was also one of the safest, she mused. Crime was rare, and people seldom bothered to lock their doors.

As Cass padded up the stone steps leading onto the terrace which stretched across the back of the house, her smile faded. Maybe the meeting would be easier if she brought Jack with her and let him work his not unconsiderable charm. Maybe she should turn right around and come back this afternoon. A retreat smacked of cowardice and would mean missing out on the water glasses, but—

She halted. Gifford was walking on the treadmill. The gym was installed in a corner room, and she could see his shadowy outline through the side window. Cautious now, she climbed the remaining steps. Was anyone with him? Imogen Sales, for example? The clinging, rail-thin Imogen. She cast a glance down at the slight swell of her stomach. If so, it would be heel-swivel and exit.

Tiptoeing across the terrace, Cass rounded the corner of the house and peeped cautiously in through sliding glass doors. Wearing only a pair of black boxer shorts, and with his muscled torso glistening with sweat, Gifford continued to pace the treadmill. Her gaze swept past him and swiftly around—there was no one else in the room—then returned.

His pace was uneven. Jerky. Laboured. Cass stepped closer, peered closer. From the knee down, his left leg was withered and misshapen. Angry scars snaked across discoloured and partly puckered skin. She frowned. His ankle appeared to have been mashed, then reconstructed—but reconstructed awkwardly.

All of a sudden, Gifford saw her. He cursed beneath his breath. He had believed he was alone. He needed to be alone. He did not want to be watched, examined…and pitied.

Stepping off the machine, he groped for a walking stick which he had propped up nearby and hobbled to the glass doors. He yanked one open.

'You make a habit of snooping?' he enquired.

'No, I—'

'You thought you'd sneak up on me?' He glared down at her, his grey eyes as cold and metallic as steel. 'I told you to telephone before you came round.'

'Did you?'

'*Yes.*'

'I'm sorry, I forgot.'

'You can't have much of a memory!'

'Galloping amnesia, and I apologise,' Cass said steadily. 'However, there's no need to go ballistic.' Her gaze dipped down. 'What's happened to your leg?'

'It makes you feel queasy?' he demanded.

'No.'

Gifford grunted. 'I bet.'

'You're speaking to someone who spent many teenage hours sitting in cinemas being scared out of her wits by aliens, creatures from black pits and the living dead. If you had entrails spewing or oozed green slime, I might be tempted to wince. But a mauled leg? Pah, it's nothing.'

Despite himself he laughed, his anger draining. 'I was in a car crash,' he said and, limping over to sit on a high-backed chair, he started to pull on his jeans.

Cass felt a wash of tenderness. Eighteen months ago, Gifford had been fit and active, a perfect specimen of physical manhood. She remembered how he had looked in the shower—firm-bodied and smooth-limbed. She also recalled running beside him through the early-

morning streets of London. Then his step had been sure
and his stride strong, but now—

Walking into the room, she watched him stand and
draw up his zip. Now she knew what it was he had been
hiding yesterday. She cast him a frowning glance. Yet
he could not have imagined that he would be able to
conceal his disability for long.

'A crash was what you were referring to when you
said you'd been unwell?' she asked.

Gifford nodded. 'I spent time in hospital.'

'How much time?'

'Almost five months. My leg was shattered, and fixing
it proved to be a lengthy business.' Lifting a white towel,
he began to blot the trickles of sweat from his throat and
shoulders. 'At one point there was talk of amputation.'

'Oh, no!'

His smile was off-centre. 'My reaction exactly.'

'It must've been quite a crash.'

'A biggie,' he said, and she glimpsed a dark world of
torment in his eyes. 'The car left the road, shot through
a stream and slammed into a rock face. The bodywork
buckled and I ended up with my leg pierced by metal
splinters and my foot twisted almost double beneath a
pedal. We were a fair distance from a town, so although
a following motorist rang the emergency services—
thank God—it took a while before they arrived. And
then I had to be cut out of the wreckage.'

'You were driving?' Cass enquired.

'I was.'

'You said "we". Was anyone else hurt?'

Gifford shook his head. 'Imogen was shaken, but
amazingly she escaped without a scratch, and there was
no other vehicle involved. Imogen is Imogen Sales,' he
said, slowly circling the towel over the curls of dark hair
on his chest. 'She's—'

'An actress. I know. I once saw a picture of the two of you in a trade journal.' She wished he would finish drying himself and put on a shirt. The rhythmic rubbing at his torso was creating pangs of arousal inside her, edgy and elemental. 'I've never seen anything in the papers about you being in a crash and no one at Dexter's has ever mentioned it,' Cass went on, with a frown. 'Not Stephen. Nor Ron Myers.'

Ron Myers was the middle-aged American who had been sent over to run the company. Although Gifford had spoken of the two of them meeting again, it had not happened. Whether he had decided to keep the Atlantic Ocean between them or had simply become involved in other business acquisitions she did not know, but Ron Myers had handled the subsequent Dexter take-over in total. And it was Ron who, whilst preserving the legacy of the brand name, was revitalising sales and trouncing the competition.

'I didn't relish the media descending so I asked Bruce and my family and friends to keep quiet. Ron knows about the accident, as do the staff in Boston, but he may not have told Stephen. I understand their relationship is a long way from buddy-buddy.'

'Stephen doesn't take easily to being sidelined,' Cass said, then adopted a tone which was intended to sound conversational and unconcerned. 'Is Imogen with you now?'

'No.' Frowning, he hooked the towel over the back of the chair. 'The relationship was brief.'

'Like ours,' she could not resist saying.

A beat went by before he answered. 'I guess.'

'Do you have a new partner living with you here?' she asked lightly.

'Who am I supposed to be, Don Juan?' Gifford demanded, with a flash of anger. 'No, I'm alone. I assume you came to collect the glasses and—' He paused and his eyes dipped to her leotard and the smooth curves of her breasts which were exposed by the low-cut neck. As well as his leg, the accident had also seemed to flatten his libido, yet right now his hormones were jumping like beans on a trampoline. 'To work out?'

'Well…yes.'

'So get busy,' he instructed, and, picking up the walking stick, he limped towards the door. 'I'll find the tumblers.'

As he disappeared, Cass shimmied out of her shorts and climbed astride the exercise bicycle. She started to pedal. Had Gifford used a cane when he had walked to the restaurant yesterday? she wondered. She had not noticed one, but she had not been looking.

She frowned. If his had been the only vehicle involved, how had the accident happened? On their business trip he had taken turns at the wheel, and had been a safe and capable driver, despite driving on the left-hand side.

Her speed increased. She really wanted to hate Gifford, she thought, but she couldn't. He was articulate, funny and uncompromisingly male, which were the reasons why she had fallen for him in the first place. And now—now she felt a deep sympathy.

'I couldn't find a box,' he said, coming back into the room a few minutes later, 'but they should be safe enough in here.' He showed her the plastic bags which he carried, one in each hand. 'I've wrapped the glasses in kitchen towel, so— Hell!'

As he stepped forward, his leg gave way and he stumbled. Cass leapt from the bike. He had returned without his cane, and his arms were starting to flail, the plastic bags swaying. She jumped in front of him, slamming her hands flat against his shoulders.

'Care-careful,' she panted, holding him steady and keeping him upright.

He looked down at her, and all of a sudden she was aware of the heat of his skin beneath her palms, the muscular width of his shoulders, their flesh-and-blood proximity. Gifford was aware of their proximity, too. His eyes had slid to the impetuous rise and fall of her breasts at the neckline of her leotard, and he seemed riveted.

She stepped back, taking the plastic bags from him and putting them down.

'You're all right?' she asked.

He nodded. 'I must've tripped on something.'

'Could be,' Cass said, though she did not believe him. 'I'll fetch you your cane.'

'No need,' he barked.

'OK, but don't get snappy.'

'Was I snappy? I do apologise.' He frowned, and when he next spoke he had dropped his ironic tone. 'Yes, I'd like my cane, please. It's next door in the kitchen.'

The man who had been at ease with himself and so easy in the world had lost his bearings, Cass thought as she walked into a dream kitchen of Canadian maple units and expensive appliances. He might not be prepared to admit it, but he had yet to come to terms with his disability.

'They must be missing you at work,' she remarked as she returned to hand him the cane.

'Not that much,' Gifford replied drily. 'A couple of my assistants took over my workload when I was in hospital and did a great job. They're in charge again. Though I went back to the office for a spell,' he told her, and frowned. 'I returned too early, and now my doctor's insisting that I relax and concentrate on strengthening my leg for a couple more months—then it'll be back to normal. And my life'll get back on track.'

Cass swung him a look. Who was he trying to kid? Her or himself? The action hero would never be as active again.

'Were you finished on the bike?' he asked.

She checked her watch and saw that it was fast approaching noon.

'No, but I must go. Today's a tour party day and I help with the waitressing.' She hesitated. She had intended to talk to him about Jack, but the surprise of his injury had knocked it out of her head. 'Plus,' she added, with a cool, level look, 'I have to feed the baby.'

Gifford's dark brows lowered. 'Baby?' he said, his tone abruptly guarded. 'What baby?'

'Jack.' In an unconscious move Cass shifted her stance, lifting her chin. 'My baby.'

There was a long, still, heavy silence.

'Stephen dropped hints,' he said slowly, 'but I decided that, once again, he must be fantasising.'

He had rarely felt jealous, but now he experienced a bolt of jealousy which seemed to tear a hole in his chest. What a fool he had been to end their relationship. OK, he had felt bothered about it and unsure, but—

'Stephen?' she asked, puzzled.

'We spoke on the phone—oh, it must've been at the end of last year. I rang to ask how you were—'

'He never mentioned it.'

'He said that you'd moved into his apartment.'

Cass nodded. 'At short notice the landlord decided he wanted to sell the house where I rented my flat, and Stephen had plenty of room, so he suggested I join him.'

'Room for you and—Jack?'

'That's right.'

'Jack—his son.' Gifford rubbed hard at his temple. 'You must go.'

Dazed, she looked at him. Jack—*Stephen's* son? What was he talking about?

'Go?' she echoed.

'To feed the baby and help with the tour party.'

'Oh. Right. Yes.' Blindly, she reached for her shorts and stepped into them. Then she picked up the bags containing the glasses.

'Ciao,' he said.

'Um—ciao,' Cass replied.

CHAPTER THREE

CASS'S gaze travelled from Edith who sat in shocked disbelief on one side of the table and across to Kirk Weber who smiled a toothpaste-white smile on the other. There was one sure-fire way of forgetting about your own troubles, Cass thought ruefully—being hit with someone else's.

Because Jack had slept on for once—and because she had lain awake half the night trying to make sense of what Gifford had said the previous day—she had arisen late. After feeding the baby his breakfast while she ate hers, she had spent an industrious hour bringing the restaurant's accounts book up to date. A playful time with her son had followed, until his lids had begun to droop and she had put him down to rest. She had been wondering whether to give the corner bar a quick spring clean when the South African had appeared.

His request for a powwow had filled her with a voluptuous sense of relief. At long last, she had thought, his funds must be in place. But within minutes her relief was whining away like air from a fast deflating balloon.

'You can't do this!' Edith protested, appealing to Kirk. She swung Cass a stricken look. 'He can't, can he?'

Cass placed her hand over the other woman's hand. Edith was a natural born follower who tended to flap at the first sign of trouble. When Oscar had been alive she had depended on him to organise and make things right, and now she was depending on her. Cass frowned. She longed to be able to say that she could fix matters, but her touch was the only comfort she could give.

'I can,' Kirk declared, in his clipped accent. He brushed a speck of lint from his black pin-striped trousers. 'I'm not made of money and I'd be an idiot to pay more.'

'I don't—' Edith bleated.

'Take it or leave it,' he said, his white smile gleaming out from the smooth bronze of his face.

'The Forgotten Eden has charm and is in a beautiful location,' Cass told him determinedly. 'The cottages need to be refurbished, but—'

Kirk rose to his feet. 'I'll be back tomorrow.'

As he started to walk away, she got up from her chair and followed him.

'What you're doing is unethical,' she began, her tone stern.

He stopped and turned to her. 'Business is business.'

'This isn't business, it's sharp practice, and a dirty trick!'

Snaking an arm around her waist, the South African drew her against him. 'Now, now, my lovely Cassie, don't take it personally,' he said.

She froze. His grip was tight, flattening her breasts against his chest. The cloying fumes of aftershave filled her nostrils.

'Let me go,' Cass ordered, in a low, fierce voice.

'Sweetheart—'

'Let me go!' The words were snapped out.

His smile still shining in what seemed a stay-pressed fixture, Kirk released her. 'I'd like us to be friends,' he said, straightening the deep pink tie which toned with the pink of his candy-striped shirt.

'And I'd like you to play by the rules!' she retaliated.

He seemed about to murmur glib, soothing words

when his gaze abruptly lifted and he looked beyond her. 'You have a visitor. I'll be back tomorrow for your answer, at five-fifteen,' he said, and strode off.

What did she do now? Cass wondered as the engine of the Jeep which he had parked on the yard roared into life. What *could* she do? She had promised her uncle that she would help his girlfriend, but instead she had allowed her to be ambushed, and now Edith was in grave danger of being cheated.

Abruptly recalling the reference to a visitor, she turned to see Gifford coming across the lawn. She frowned. It had occurred to her that his distaste for being seen to limp might keep him, hermit-like, at Maison d'Horizon, but he was leaning on his cane and walking with care. He wore a chambray shirt with the sleeves rolled up above his elbows, old jeans and a pair of tinted aviator glasses. His appearance was casual, yet he possessed far more natural style than the formally attired and dress-conscious Kirk.

Cass rubbed at the headache which was starting to throb behind her temples. She wished he had stayed at the villa. It had been a rough enough morning already, and the last thing she needed was to have to cope with yet more trauma.

As he mounted the short flight of steps which led into the restaurant, an instinct to help propelled her forward.

'I don't require a nursemaid,' Gifford said, grasping the wooden balustrade and heaving himself up.

He smiled as he spoke, but the warning was there. What he did require, Cass thought pungently, was a notice on his back saying 'Fragile—handle with care'.

Removing his dark glasses, he snapped them closed and slid them into his top pocket.

'Who was the guy you were cuddling up to just now?' he enquired.

'Kirk Weber, though—'

'The guy who's buying the Forgotten Eden? I thought you reckoned he was good-looking? He has the over-laundered looks of a guy in a TV mini-series.' His lip curled. 'But if that's what floats your boat—' All of a sudden, he noticed Edith sitting at the table towards the back of the restaurant. Her shoulders were slumped and she had her head buried in her hands. 'Is something wrong?' he enquired.

The older woman looked up, her large brown eyes glistening with tears. 'Everything!' she wailed.

'When Kirk arrived this morning we believed it was all systems go,' Cass explained as they started to make their way towards her. 'But then he announced that, al-though the money is available, he isn't prepared to pay the full price for the Forgotten Eden.'

'How much is he prepared to pay?' Gifford enquired.

'Half.'

He swore. 'That's one hell of a reduction.'

'It's peanuts and an insult,' she said, frowning. 'Be-fore Oscar put the property up for sale he had it valued, and the asking price is the valuation price. The price also includes all fixtures and fittings. OK, there's nothing of great value, but they're worth something.'

Reaching Edith, Gifford pulled out a chair beside her and sat down. 'Hadn't the guy already agreed to buy at the full amount?' he asked.

Cass bobbed her head. 'Yes, but when I protested he said that if we checked we'd find he's committed to nothing on paper which is legally binding.'

'Is that right?'

'I can't say for sure without speaking to the solicitors, but I suspect Kirk's much too cute not to know exactly where he stands. Though even if he was committed to paying the full price and Edith wanted to sue him for breach of contract she couldn't afford it.'

'Not in a hundred years,' the older woman confirmed unhappily.

'I asked Kirk if he still wanted the property,' Cass continued, taking a seat on the other side of the table, 'or whether this was a way of wriggling out, but he insisted he does want to buy—at the right price.'

'He told us the right price was fifty per cent, and smiled when he said it!' Edith recalled, her emotions wavering between righteous indignation and tearful despair. 'He also reckoned I should be grateful.'

'Grateful?' Gifford asked.

'Kirk said no one else is showing a flicker of interest,' Cass explained, 'and that Edith should get smart and grab what he's offering before he decides that fifty per cent is too generous.'

'He's given us a day to decide,' the older woman said. Her fingers plucked at the gold chain which she wore around her neck, twisting and worrying. 'Perhaps I should accept half.'

Gifford shook his head. 'No.'

'It may be peanuts,' Edith fretted, 'but it's better than nothing and I need the money. I *need* it,' she declared on a sob, then she tilted her head and sniffed. 'Must take a look at the chicken curry,' she mumbled, and hurried away into the kitchen.

'The guy's pulling a stunt,' Gifford declared.

Cass nodded. 'And I should've seen it coming. Edith may've thought he was wonderful, but I found him a touch too smooth, too amiable. ''One may smile, and smile, and be a villain'', to quote someone in Shakespeare.'

'Hamlet,' he said.

Putting her elbows on the table, she rested her chin

on her hands and looked bleakly across at him. 'It's obvious now that the claim of having difficulty in rounding up his funds was a lie, and that for four weeks Kirk's been keeping us dangling and making us sweat. And for four weeks he's been checking that he's the only bidder.'

'I'm afraid so.'

'Instead of taking it for granted that the transaction was watertight, I ought to have visited the solicitors myself and checked it through with them. I knew Edith didn't have a clue,' she said. 'I should've also found out more about Kirk. Demanded a character reference.'

'It isn't your fault that the guy's a chancer,' he said and, reaching out a hand, he drew his knuckles down the softness of her cheek. 'So stop beating yourself up.'

Cass frowned. Whilst his touch comforted, it had also sent her nerves zinging.

'But I should've known!' she protested.

'Known he'd double-cross you, resort to strong-arm tactics and attempt to pressurise? Impossible. Kirk made you sweat, so what you do now is make him sweat.'

'How?'

Gifford sat back. Ever since it had become clear that she hadn't been snuggling up to the South African, he had been filled with a need to touch her. But by touching her he was putting himself through an exquisite kind of agony. And yet, perversely, to touch her, to want to try and comfort her, seemed so damn natural.

'When the guy turns up tomorrow you tell him he can take his fifty per cent and—for want of a better phrase—go stuff it. That'll call his bluff.'

'But suppose he isn't bluffing?' Cass said, worry gnawing inside her. 'If Edith passes up the chance to sell now, even at half price, a long time could go by before another buyer happens along. Years! After all, it's not

everyone who'd want to become mine host at the
Forgotten Eden.'

'Just a clown who's as nutty as a fruitcake?' he suggested.

The ghost of a smile flickered across her lips.
'Maybe…and yet Kirk isn't a clown.'

'No, he's a two-faced bastard who's trying it on.'

'You think.'

'Don't you?'

She frowned. 'Yes.'

'Which means he can be played at his own game,'
Gifford stated. 'Believe me.'

'I do,' Cass said.

She knew from working with him in the past that he
was an astute and level-headed businessman, with a
mind like a steel trap. She cast him a look. Whatever
his other failings, she respected his commercial judge-
ment, and was grateful for his support now. So grateful
that she felt an infantile urge to climb onto his knee, rest
her head against his shoulder and whimper.

'Why is Edith so desperate for the money?' he enquired.

'Because she's bought a house at Grand Anse and—'

'Grand Anse is the little seaside village which I came
through on my way from the airport?' he interrupted.

'That's right. It has a church, school, shops and some
pretty bungalows.'

'Edith bought a house on the strength of Kirk's offer?'

'Yes. She went straight out—'

'You let her do that?' he rapped out, cutting in again.
'I thought you had more sense. Hell, Cass, you knew
the previous sale had fallen through.'

'I didn't let her,' she slammed back, his criticism
making her testy. Sit on his knee? Forget it. 'Edith arranged to buy the house without telling me and before I

arrived. Apparently she's always admired it, and as soon as she's free of the Forgotten Eden she'll move in there with her sister. And she financed the purchase with a loan,' she completed.

Gifford muttered an expletive.

'Edith's an innocent soul,' she went on, 'and she seems to have believed that the money for the Forgotten Eden would materialise within a couple of weeks. Of course, she's had to pay one month's instalment and interest on the loan already. That made serious inroads into her bank account, and she can't afford to pay for much longer. And if she tries to sell the bungalow that might take ages, too.'

He rubbed at his jaw with thoughtful fingers. 'Even so, you should advise Kirk that his fifty per cent is unacceptable and that he must cough up the full price. It's a gamble and nothing is guaranteed, but—'

'It's what you'd do?'

'Yup.'

'Then I'll suggest it to Edith.'

He arched a brow. 'Edith will agree?'

Cass half smiled. 'Probably.'

'Definitely. She relies on you to deal with things for her—like Stephen,' he said, and frowned. 'Does Kirk always dress as if he's stepped out of a tailor's shop window or come straight from the office?'

'He has done whenever I've seen him.' She glanced down at her pale blue sleeveless vest and frayed Bermuda shorts. 'He makes me feel such a scruff.'

'An appealingly sexy scruff,' Gifford said.

His drawling comment and the look in his eyes reminded her of the past—of their affair—and, all of a sudden, her own troubles were no longer forgotten. Now they clamoured and shrieked in her head.

The silence from the buggy, which she had settled

behind a rattan screen at the rear of the restaurant, indicated that Jack was asleep. How long would he remain asleep? she wondered. Might Gifford ask to see him? Would he recognise the child as his? But when they reached that point she wanted to be calm, composed and in a robust frame of mind.

'What brings you over here?' she enquired, hoping that his visit would be brief. 'Have you popped round to borrow a cup of sugar, as neighbours are supposed to do?'

He shook his head. 'I'm here to have lunch.'

'Oh.'

'You sound a little thin on enthusiasm,' Gifford remarked. 'I know I have a few shortcomings, but—'

'A few?'

'OK, several. But, whilst I don't profess to be a shining saint, I am not that much of a blackguard.'

'In your opinion,' Cass said sweetly.

'In my opinion,' he acknowledged, then continued. 'The box of groceries has arrived so I am able to feed myself, but you mentioned that Edith was a good cook and I thought I'd sample one of her meals.'

Turning, he surveyed the menu which was chalked on a blackboard propped up alongside the bar. He had also come over because he had felt a need to see Cass again, but there was no way he would confess to that.

'I'm torn between the curry which smells so good and the tiger prawns in tomato dressing with millionaire's salad,' he said. 'Which do you recommend?'

As the population of the Seychelles had originally come from the continents of Africa, Europe and Asia and freely intermingled, so the cuisine was an amalgam of Creole and French, with Indian spices and a Chinese influence tossed in. All of it was delicious.

'Both,' she replied.

'That's real helpful,' Gifford said, and cocked his head. There was the sound of a vehicle drawing to a halt in the yard. 'The customers are starting to pour in.'

Cass gave a wry smile. 'If only.'

'Look who I picked up on the road.' Veronica giggled, walking into the restaurant a couple of minutes later with her arm linked possessively through Jules's. 'My favourite man.'

The young barman disentangled himself. 'But I have to leave my favourite woman and open a few beer crates,' he declared, and strode off towards the swing doors.

'See you later,' Veronica crooned, wiggling her fingers.

As he passed them, Jules raised his eyes to the ceiling. The divorcée was becoming much too clingy, plus she was old enough to be his mother.

Instead of making for her usual table which was close to the bar, Veronica took a detour.

'Good morning,' she said, arriving to smile at Cass and then gaze interestedly down at Gifford.

'Hi,' he replied.

'This is Veronica Milne,' Cass said, introducing them.

The redhead appeared to have ransacked the rails of her dress shop before setting off on holiday, for every time she visited the Forgotten Eden she was dressed in a different outfit. Today she wore a black lace halter-neck and white satin bell-bottom trousers. Whilst she did not wish to be uncharitable, it was, Cass thought, a somewhat over-the-top outfit for the time and place.

'You're lunching here?' Veronica asked Gifford.

'I am.'

'Alone?'

There was a pause. 'That's right.'

'Me, too.' The redhead shone a coy, little-girl smile at him. 'Perhaps I should join you?'

Gifford looked across at Cass. Get me out of this, *please*—the message was written in capital letters in his eyes.

Cass shone him a seraphic smile. Whilst he might not be entirely the villain she had imagined, he had enchanted her for two wondrous months, taken her into his bed—then dumped her.

'What a splendid idea,' she declared.

Both diners chose the tiger prawn salad, but, whereas Veronica toyed with hers, Gifford wolfed his down and asked for his cheque. Because Marquise's waitressing duties only covered tour party days and the occasional evening, Cass was on duty, and the look he flung her as he handed over a wad of rupee notes was murderous.

'Your change, *sir*,' she called as he grabbed up his cane and limped down the steps in a burst of astonishing speed.

'Keep it,' he yelled back.

She chuckled. Throughout the meal, Veronica had conducted an eager flirtation which had included the batting of eyelids, simpering smiles, twee come-ons—the works. She had not seemed to notice that the flirtation was one-sided nor that Gifford—who had started off by taking a polite if strained interest in her non-stop chatter—was soon doing a good imitation of mean, moody and magnificent.

'Such a nice man,' the redhead declared as she clambered onto a high stool at the bar. She reached over to squeeze Jules's hand. 'But you're nicer.'

Although the young barman made no sound, Cass heard his groan.

The monitor was turned to full volume and stuck upright in the sand. Kicking off her flip-flops, Cass drew up her bare legs and wrapped her arms around them. Darkness had fallen. The heat of the day had gone and the air stroked across her skin like warm chiffon. Lamps in the deserted restaurant behind her cast long beams of pale light. High above in the black sky, a melon moon glowed and a million silver stars twinkled. The only sound was the soft suck of the ocean at the shore. It was the perfect tropical night.

She rested her chin on her knees. The perfect night after an action-packed day. A day when Kirk Weber had dropped his bombshell, when Veronica had persisted in staying all afternoon to play with Jack and into the evening to pester Jules, when a bunch of holidaymakers had unexpectedly arrived to down tankards of the locally brewed lager, eat a hearty dinner and carouse. A day when there had been too much happening for her to take time out and concentrate.

But she needed to concentrate. She needed to think about how best to break the news to Gifford that he was her son's father. The revelation would be a pivotal moment which could affect his attitude in the future, and so it was vital that she get it right.

Cass watched the tiny fluorescent fish which tumbled like so many silver coins at the edge of the ocean. For eighteen months she had believed Gifford to be a rat with a stone in place of a heart, but he wasn't, because he had not known about the baby. Why hadn't he known?

She had sent him two letters. The first, which had advised him of her pregnancy, she had given to Stephen who had been visiting Boston on business. The second, informing Gifford that he had an eight-pound-one-ounce son, had been mailed to him, marked 'private and confidential', at the Tait-Hill offices.

She had always assumed he had read both letters, but he must have decided he had no interest in reading anything from a woman whom he regarded as history and torn them up. Stephen would have said the first came from her and Gifford would have recognised her handwriting on the second envelope.

Cass pulled at the fraying threads of her Bermudas. His failure to reply had seemed an apt sequel to him ditching her. She had felt so sure he didn't want anything to do with the baby, but she was not sure now.

Nor was she sure about Stephen having 'dropped hints' which had implied that he was Jack's father. Had he been joking or might the young man have been involved in a deliberate deception? A line cut between her brows. Stray past comments—comments which she had dismissed as inconsequential—now made the latter a possibility. As did the fact that Gifford could not be aware of Jack's age.

When she made the revelation, how would he react? she wondered. Would he be smitten with fatherly feelings and insist on playing a role in the little boy's upbringing? An active role? Might he request regular visits or a share of access? OK, he lived in the States, but jumbo jets zoomed back and forth daily.

Cass dug her toes into the sand. Whilst she desperately wanted father and son to establish a close relationship, she had to admit that the prospect of being forced to talk to Gifford on the phone and meet with him, year after year, was unsettling. Yes, Jack needed his father, but she shied away from the thought of, perhaps, being informed some time that Gifford had, after all, decided to marry and, perhaps, being expected to meet his wife. Yet, for Jack's sake, she would grin and bear it.

She was brooding over the scenario of their lives necessarily overlapping when she lifted her head and lis-

tened. There was the splash of water. Narrowing her
eyes, she looked down the slope of silvered sand and
out at the inky, moonlit ocean. A man was swimming
in the middle of the cove. With arms moving in a fluent
crawl, he was making for the shore. As he came closer,
her toes dug deeper into the sand. The swimmer was
Gifford.

Had he noticed her sitting here? Presumably. And he
would certainly see her if she made a dash back to her
cottage. So she would stay.

She watched as he stopped swimming, stood upright
and began to wade out through the shallows.

Her heartbeat accelerated. In a pair of black stretch
swimtrunks, and with water glossing his body, he looked
like a sea god. The drag of his leg did not matter. He
was all muscular, all masterful, all male.

'That was terrific,' Gifford said as he came up the
beach towards her. He flicked back his head, clearing
spikes of wet dark hair from his eyes and sending a spray
of drops flying. 'The water's so deep and clear. User-
friendly.'

'In the cove—but everywhere else along this part of
the coast it's shallow and seaweedy. I only just noticed
you,' she said. 'Have you been swimming for long?'

'About half an hour. I went out round the headland.'

'Alone and at night?' Cass protested. 'That's dangerous. You could've suffered cramp and got into difficul-
ties. Or had a close encounter with a shark, though they
usually stay much further out.'

'But I didn't.' He lifted a brow. 'If I had, would you
have cared?'

She flushed, aware of how concerned she had
sounded—and how concerned she had felt. 'Of course.
After all, you are a member of the human race.'

'Gee, thanks,' Gifford said drily.

'How about suffering indigestion?' she asked, and tilted him a mischievous smile. 'You did gallop through your lunch.'

'I've escaped that, too,' he said, going past her to collect a towel which she saw had been draped on the low branch of a tree. His cane lay on the sand beneath it. 'Though Veronica would give anyone a sore gut. Not only does she continually gush, but—' he shuddered '—she's a man-eater.'

'You were scared?'

He returned to stand beside her and begin to dry himself. 'Terrified. Give her half a chance and she'd have the pants off a guy as soon as look at him.'

Cass laughed. 'That's why you sprinted off as soon as you could?'

'I didn't exactly sprint,' he said, with a frown, 'but yes.'

'Veronica does come on too strong, but she's newly divorced and alone.'

'OK, the woman's going through a hard time.' Gifford towelled his hair, changing the smooth jet-black cap to roughened spikes. 'However, I am not—repeat, not— eating a meal with her again. *Understand?*'

'*Understand*. Does your leg hurt?' she enquired as he bent to gingerly rub it dry. She saw him tense. 'Sorry, I guess that was a stupid question.'

'Yes, it was,' he rasped. 'Got any more?' He glared at her for a moment, then he finished his rubbing and straightened. 'It doesn't hurt so much these days as ache,' he said, his tone calmer. 'It's aching like fury now.'

'You have been swimming for half an hour,' Cass reminded him.

'Yup,' he said, and grinned. 'That's the longest I've swum since the crash.'

'Do you swim back home?'

Gifford lowered himself down onto the sand beside her. He was on the point of spreading the towel over his injured limb when his eyes met hers. A muscle knotted and unknotted in his jaw—then he laid the towel aside.

'My doctor recommended it, but—'

'You don't because you think the sight of your leg'll have the other bathers giving blood-curdling screams and running for cover?' Cass suggested, when he frowned out at the sea.

His gaze cut back to her. 'Do you have to be so damn smart?' he demanded, his tone jokey yet laced with irritation.

'Sorry, I can't help it.'

'I went to the pool a few times, but I was conscious of people sneaking glances, and then a couple who recognised me began to commiserate about my once having been such a good skier.'

'So you became uptight and decided you wouldn't go swimming again? That's stupid,' Cass said.

A nerve throbbed in his temple. 'I appreciate your candour.'

'No, you don't. You consider I'm making interfering observations about something which is none of my business, and you're hopping mad.'

'I'm not hopping mad,' Gifford said, squeezing the words out. He indicated the sea. 'Are you intending to swim?'

She shook her head. 'I'm on the beach because I didn't feel ready to go to bed, and—' she hesitated '—because I wanted to think.'

'Edith's babysitting?'

'No, I have the alarm. See?' She showed him the monitor. 'One cry and—' she looked back at her cottage '—I'm there in seconds.'

'When you were telling me about how you'd come to the Seychelles, you said you'd wanted a change of scene.' Scooping up a handful of sand, he let it sieve out between his long fingers. 'You wanted to get away from Stephen?'

'Right,' Cass said shortly.

After a busy day, she was tired and in no mood to spring her surprise on him. Though she did not intend to spring. The most prudent course of action must be to set a calm mood, then try to drip-feed clues which would ease him into the idea of fatherhood. And when he had been sufficiently eased she would cross her fingers, weigh her words—and hope for the best.

'The two of you have hit a bad patch?' Gifford enquired.

'Not exactly; we're still friends. But when I leave here—and I've promised Edith I'll stay until the Forgotten Eden has been sold—I shall be moving out of his apartment.'

'Your affair is over?'

'There was never an affair.'

His head swung round and he frowned at her. 'No?'

'No,' Cass replied, thinking that to drop clues and yet avoid an outright announcement was a nerve-racking juggling act. 'Stephen had been keen to have me as a flatmate, with my own room,' she inserted, 'when I was pregnant. But once Jack appeared his enthusiasm dipped.'

'He didn't like being woken up in the night?' Gifford suggested.

'Hated it. Nor did he like the baby crying during the day or having his kitchen draped with washing. Stephen's house-proud, and as Jack grew bigger and began to touch things, dribble and sometimes be sick on the carpet he became more and more disapproving. So when I return I shall go and stay—temporarily—with my father in Cambridge.'

'Temporarily?'

'I have money saved, and I intend to buy a house in the seaside town in Devon where my brother and his wife live, and provide bed and breakfast for holiday-makers. That way, Jack won't be a latchkey kid,' she explained. 'And he's my priority.'

'So you've quit your position with Dexter's?'

'I left six weeks ago, just before I came out here,' she told him.

'I thought the idea of you taking a sabbatical seemed odd,' he muttered.

'Because Stephen pressed me to continue I agreed to work part-time after Jack was born, but I always hated leaving him at the nursery.'

'Stephen wanted you to continue because he knows he's incapable of doing his job without you,' Gifford said caustically.

She nodded. 'He'll find it difficult on his own.'

'Perhaps he'll decide to leave the firm—to the enormous relief of everyone.'

'He has spoken of taking a course in interior design, so it's possible. Though his father'll be furious if there's no longer a Dexter at Dexter's,' Cass said, with a rueful grimace.

'Your father will be pleased to have you living with him for a while,' Gifford said, remembering how she had told him that her father, a widower, lived on his own.

'Yes, though half the time he'll forget I'm there,' she said, and smiled. 'Dad's the original absent-minded professor.'

'Has he found himself a new wife?'

She laughed at such an unlikely idea. 'No!' Although

it was ten years since her mother had died, her father had never looked at another woman. 'He and my mother were devoted, and now he's devoted to her memory. He always will be.'

'He's not like my old man,' Gifford said, and his expression tightened. 'He's had three wives—my mother was the first—and a string of girlfriends in between. When I visited him as a kid, I had no idea who was going to open his front door.'

'I didn't know that,' she said, in surprise.

'When we were together before we rarely mentioned our families. We talked business and gazed into each other's eyes, but much of our personal relationship was red-hot passion and riotous couplings.' Lifting his hand, he ran a fingertip down her bare arm, awakening all her nerves. 'It was earth-moving stuff.'

'For the short time it lasted,' Cass said crisply.

'It should've lasted for longer.' His fingertip traced patterns across the fine bones of her wrist. 'I wish it had.'

She swung him a withering look. 'Pause for hollow laughter.'

'You don't believe me? You should,' Gifford said, and he leant forward and kissed her.

The touch of his lips was electric. It brought every pore and particle of her springing alive. She quivered. Deep inside, she felt an instinctive recognition of bodies. A dangerous recognition. Raising her hands to his shoulders, Cass made to push away, but at that moment his lips parted hers and she felt the moist caress of his tongue.

Her pulses raced. Her heart knocked against her ribs. Her pushing hands stilled. Eighteen months ago, Gifford had been able to arouse her with what had seemed insolent ease, and he was arousing her now. Her breasts were swelling, the honey-brown nipples tightening, and a bitter-sweet ache had started to pulse between her thighs. She had not made love for so long—not since they had last made love, Cass thought dazedly—and she was frustrated. But also, whilst it was supremely aggravating, she had to admit that she still cared for him.

'Don't you wish we'd been together longer?' he enquired, drawing back.

It would have taken a thumbscrew, a ducking stool and wild horses to get her to confess to him that she regretted the brevity of their relationship…and its end.

'You're joking!' she said.

Gifford looked at her in silence, then, easing her gently down, he laid her on the sand and bent over her. As he kissed her again, her hands slid up over his shoulders and around his neck. She knew her submission contradicted what she had just said and made no sense, but she could not help herself. He was half lying on top of her, and the pressure of his mouth, the weight of his body, the intimate push of his manhood seemed so familiar, and yet so new. And profoundly intoxicating.

He shifted, easing away sideways to allow himself more freedom. As his hand closed over the fullness of her breast, Cass trembled. A heat began to grow inside her. The urge to make love gathered. His thumb was stroking across her nipple, moving relentlessly back and forth until the peak rose in straining rigidity.

'It wasn't imagination,' Gifford said, his mouth close to her mouth.

She opened her eyes. 'Sorry?'

'I'd wondered whether I'd exaggerated the chemistry which I remembered between us. I hadn't.'

'No?' she asked tremulously.

'No—and it's still potent,' he said, his voice husky. 'It's—'

'Maaah!'

As a piercing yowl rang out just a couple of feet away from their heads, she jumped. Gifford jerked back.

'What the hell—?' he protested.

'It's Jack,' she said, slithering out from beneath him and hastily scrambling up. 'He's crying.'

What had she been doing? Cass wondered frantically as she brushed sand from the seat of her Bermudas. Lust or need or, yes, fondness had carried her away, but was she a complete fool? What had happened to 'once bitten, twice shy'? And learning from her mistakes? Hadn't she sworn that her ex-lover would be kept at arm's length and their relationship would be strictly neutral?

'He's not a happy bunny,' Gifford remarked as another yowl sounded. He got to his feet. 'Is he hungry?'

'Shouldn't be. He rolls over onto his tummy, but he hasn't learned how to roll back yet, and so he wakes up, realises he's stuck and yells. That'll probably be what's happened now. I must go,' she declared, picking up the monitor.

'I'll see you home,' he said, and as she turned he slung his towel over one broad shoulder, retrieved his cane and walked with her. 'That was perfect timing.'

She swung him a sideways look. 'Excuse me?'

'By yelling when he did, the baby stopped us from getting too carried away. From—'

'I understand,' she cut in, not needing him to spell it out.

What she also understood, Cass thought, was that Gifford regretted their embrace. He, too, had been gripped by animal attraction, but was relieved to have been able to escape. In other words, he was giving her the elbow again. Thank goodness.

'He sounds pretty angry,' he remarked as they reached her cottage.

She gave a rueful nod of agreement. During their short

walk, Jack's yells had increased in frequency and in volume.

'Good night,' she said, and sped inside.

Crossing the shadowy living room, she swung into the tiny second bedroom. A lamp on a chest of drawers shone subdued light on a pine cot and the baby who lay on his stomach, bawling fit to bust.

'It's OK, popcorn,' Cass said softly. 'Mummy's here.'

As she bent and lifted him into her arms, he gave a shuddering sob and quietened. For a few moments she stood, savouring the weight and warmth of his small, sleep-suited body against her shoulder, then, kissing his brow, she started to lay him down.

'Back to sleep,' she murmured, but Jack let out an indignant yowl.

She was giving him another cuddle when she became aware of Gifford. He was standing in the doorway, frowning. The sight of him—the unexpectedness—sliced through her emotions like a knife.

'What do you want?' Cass asked sharply.

'I came to say that if you'd like to work out tomorrow to come round…'

His words died away. Whilst he had scant idea of babies' ages, he had expected this one to be small and helpless, lying in her arms. Instead the child was straight-backed and looked sturdy. Also, Stephen Dexter was fair-haired, but the baby was dark…like himself.

'How old is he?' he demanded.

Her heart pounded like a drum in her ears. Her nerves twanged. So much for setting a calm mood and weighing her words, Cass thought. So much for the moment being right.

'Nine months.'

Gifford stared at her, stared at the baby, and then his eyes met hers again. Chaos raged in his head.

'Oh, God,' he said. 'He's mine.'

She swallowed. 'Yes.'

He gazed at the child. Time which common sense insisted could only be seconds, but which seemed to her like hours, went by before he spoke again.

'Why didn't you tell me? I have a son, and yet for nine months you keep quiet about him. You don't bother to inform me that I'm a father. You conceal his existence. How dare you?' he raged, his voice rough and angry, and, frightened by the noise, Jack began to cry.

'Shh, popcorn, shh.' Cass rubbed the baby's back and rocked him against her. 'I did tell you,' she said, speaking in a fervent whisper. 'I wrote two letters.' Her chin tilted. Her blue eyes burned into his. 'Remember?'

'I never received any letters.'

'You didn't tear them up?'

'No.'

'Are you sure?' she challenged.

'Positive,' he grated.

'Well, I sent them. Shh,' Cass said again, rocking the baby. Perhaps it was because he could sense the tension between them, but his yells showed no sign of lessening. 'I sent the first—'

'Leave it,' Gifford interjected. 'We can't talk now. Come to the villa tomorrow morning.' He frowned at the bawling child. 'And bring him.'

CHAPTER FOUR

'WATCH out for your ears,' Cass warned. She pulled the T-shirt on over Jack's head, manoeuvred his arms out through the armholes and smoothed down his hair. Holding his hands, she stood him up in front of the mirror. 'Don't you have street cred?' she said, smiling at his reflection.

The baby bounced up and down in boisterous delight.

His T-shirt was blue and white striped, teamed with short denim dungarees which had workmanlike brass buckles on the braces, and a leather pocket-patch which proclaimed 'Hell's cherub'.

'The sun's strong, so you're to keep this on,' she told him, fitting a denim baseball cap onto his silky dark head. He made an immediate grab for the peak. 'On,' Cass repeated, and handed him a small plastic car—which proved to be a successful diversion.

As it was a tour party day, after breakfast she had set the tables, helped with the vegetables and prepared a vast bowl of tropical fruit salad. Her immediate duties done, she had told Edith that she needed to speak with Gifford.

'I'll be back well before noon,' she had assured her.

'But first you're off to get changed?'

Cass had glanced down at her baggy shirt and shorts. 'Yes.'

The other woman had chuckled, her dark eyes twinkling. 'Thought so. You two seem kind of…chummy.'

'We know each other from the past,' she had said vaguely, and sped off, reluctant to embark on an explanation which would be time-consuming and difficult.

Cass gave herself a last look in the mirror. Because she needed all the confidence she could muster for her meeting with Gifford this morning, she had shampooed her hair and made up her face with special care. So her hair swung in a polished wheat-blonde mane, her eyelids shimmered a discreet bronze, and a rosy amber glossed her lips.

She wore a white poppy-printed sundress which had shoestring straps, a close fitting waist and a skirt which swirled around her legs when she walked. The dress had been a far too expensive impulse buy, but it flattered her. It accentuated the honey-gold of her tan and—turning sideways, she cast herself a critical glance—made her look slim.

Gathering up her son, she went out of the cottage. The path to Maison d'Horizon was too steep and narrow for easy use of the pushchair, so she carried him.

Circumnavigating the lawn, Cass set off uphill. The sun filtered through the high, leafy canopy, casting rivulets of light on spreading ferns and tropical blossoms. Cicadas hummed in the trees. It was another sunny day in paradise.

'When you met your daddy last night you were screwing up your face and yelling blue murder, which was not the ideal introduction. So today you must be on your best behaviour,' she told the baby as she walked along. 'You have to be a good little boy, wow your daddy and make him love you. Understand?'

Launching himself sideways and almost out of her grasp, Jack made a lunge at a frangipani bush which they were passing. His lunge disturbed a couple of birds, which rose up into the sky.

'You're becoming a tearaway,' Cass complained, and he chuckled.

As she resettled him in her arms, she sighed. After

spending much of the night rehearsing what she was
going to say today—and second-guessing Gifford's re-
sponses—she had hoped that her mind would be cool
and clear. Yet with each step her brain seemed to grow
foggier and her nerves twisted tighter. Her summoner
had had twelve hours to get to grips with the idea of
being a father, so what kind of a reception was she going
to get?

Would he be interested in his son…or resentful?
Would his attitude be apathetic, casual? Or might he be
eager to play a responsible and ongoing part in Jack's
life? However much she, personally, shied away from
keeping in constant touch with Gifford, she hoped so.

'I wonder if your daddy'll be exercising again?' she
said to the baby, but when they reached the bungalow
the gym was empty.

A walk across the back of the house showed that the
kitchen, dining room and study were deserted, too.

Taking a side path edged by pink periwinkles which
gave onto a lawn and garden, Cass made her way along
to the front. There was no sign of life. They had not
fixed a time, but it was ten-thirty. Might Gifford still be
in bed, or could he have waited for her, lost patience,
and decided to take another swim in the cove?

As she rounded the corner, she saw that the lacquered
oak front door stood open. She rang the bell and waited.
No one appeared. She knocked and waited. Again, nothing.

'Is he out?' she asked the baby.

Jack jiggled on her hip, merrily unaware of the importance of the imminent meeting.

Stepping into a wide cream-carpeted, cream-painted
hallway, she called, 'Gifford?' There was no reply, but
in the silence she heard the faint sound of running water.

He must be washing, and the noise must have masked her arrival.

Cass hitched her son up higher. 'We'll let him know we've arrived.'

Passing antique chests and a display of watercolours which depicted typical Seychelles scenes, she walked along the hall. As the gushing of water grew louder, she stopped at an open door and looked inside. She was looking into a bedroom decorated in sophisticated pale camel and navy—camel-coloured thick pile carpet, camel and navy patterned spread on the king-size bed, matching curtains—and off the far side of the room was an *en-suite* bathroom.

Gifford was in the bathroom. He was standing sideways on to her, leaning over a basin and peering intently into a mirror. He was shaving.

'Eureka!' she said. Jack frowned, gazing at her. She walked into the bedroom and pointed. 'There.'

As she moved closer, the baby blinked, skated a look around and focused.

Cass's pulses juddered. Gifford was barefoot, and all he wore was a pair of maroon cotton boxer shorts which fitted neatly around his backside. He must have recently showered, for his dark hair was combed damply back from his brow and the odd diamond droplet of water sparkled on his shoulders. He was absorbed in frowning at his reflection, the tilting of his face and the scraping, which were necessary to remove stubble from skin.

She watched as he sliced away foam in long, smooth strokes, then washed his razor beneath the running water again. There was more slicing, another sluicing. And again. Abruptly he nodded, rinsed away slivers of foam, and checked his jaw. Turning off the tap, he turned away to reach for a towel.

As if mesmerised, her eyes travelled over the supple

length of his back. Old memories were surfacing again. Memories of how she had once licked the tip of her tongue slowly and teasingly down his spine. Of how, in the heat of lovemaking, she had clawed at his shoulders and engraved the crescent-shaped marks of her finger-nails in his flesh. Of how—

'Brrh!' Jack blew a noisy raspberry.

Startled, Gifford swivelled and saw them. His stomach muscles clenched. Yesterday evening when he had seen the child, he had felt no connection with him. No genetic link. No emotional pull. Nothing. Except curiosity.

And why should he? he had thought later as he had sat on the terrace, sipping whisky. He had not been pres-ent at his birth, and for the first nine months of the kid's life he had never set eyes on him. Which meant, he had decided, that it was too late for him to feel—truly and deeply *feel*—anything. The time for bonding had gone.

But it was not too late. The emotions were churning inside him now. Emotions which he was unable to de-fine, but which made him want to shout out loud and tell the world that this baby—this healthy, handsome boy—was *his* son.

'I didn't sneak up,' Cass said, suddenly conscious of how she had walked into the house and stood and watched him. 'I rang the bell and shouted, but—'

'I didn't hear you. I thought I would, which is why I left the front door open,' he said, and walked forward. He grinned at the baby. 'You look a darn sight happier this morning.'

For a long moment, Jack eyed him solemnly from beneath the peak of his cap, and then he stretched out his arms towards him.

Cass felt a jolt of surprise. Although the child was easy and affectionate with people he knew, he had a wariness of strangers and, in particular, of men. So was blood thicker than water? Whether it was or not, he seemed eager to be with his father.

'Your son,' she said, lifting Jack forward.

Gifford hesitated. 'My son,' he said gravely, and took him from her.

As she looked at them—the tall, well-made man holding the baby a little awkwardly against his bare chest—her throat constricted. Gifford was gazing down at Jack in the same besotted, wondering way she had gazed at him when he had been newborn. Like her, he seemed awed by the miracle of creation and the thought that he had helped make this new small human being.

'You're a great little kid,' he said hoarsely, and when he glanced across at her she saw that his eyes were wet with unshed tears.

A joyful relief leapt inside her. The absent father was not indifferent or hostile. He had accepted his son and already showed signs of caring. It was a good start. A thankfully promising start. The seeds of them forming a worthwhile relationship had been sown.

'I think so,' Cass said, smiling, 'but I'm biased.'

Gifford smiled back. 'Me, too,' he said, and an understanding passed between them—the unspoken acknowledgement that they were linked by Jack and to Jack, *their* child. 'I'm in pain,' he muttered, all of a sudden.

'Your leg's hurting?' she said in dismay.

'No, Jack's grabbed the hairs on my chest and he's pulling and—' he grimaced '—it's *murder*.'

Cass laughed. 'So you distract him.' Removing his denim cap, she held it out to the baby who released his grip on the whorls of dark hair and took hold. 'Were you just getting up?'

Gifford shook his head. 'I've been up since seven.'

And I was awake most of the night, he added silently,

thinking about the implications of having a son—and about you.

'But when I was eating breakfast I suddenly thought about Edith and the trouble she'd gotten herself into with the Forgotten Eden,' he continued. 'It occurred to me that an idiot's guide to buying and selling property might be useful, and perhaps an idiot's guide to running a small business. Steady on,' he protested, for Jack was flapping the cap wildly around. 'So I went into the study to jot down a few notes and got sidetracked.'

'You intend to write these guides yourself?' she asked.

'Yes, though first I intend to assemble an outline to show a publisher. It's just an idea, and might not come to anything, but it'll give me something to do while I'm here.'

'I didn't think you'd last long doing nothing,' Cass said wryly.

He shrugged. 'It's better than watching Bugs Bunny on satellite television.'

And it'll be a diversion from endlessly chewing over our relationship, he said, in his head. 'Would you like a coffee?'

'Please. Shall I take Jack while you get dressed?' she suggested.

Gifford nodded, handed over the child and crossed to a chest of drawers. Taking out a pair of denims and a short-sleeved indigo-coloured shirt, he put them on. He tucked the shirt into his jeans and then shepherded her out into the hall and along to the kitchen.

'I figured Jack would want something to play with while we're talking,' he said, and showed her three bright yellow tennis balls in a plastic tube. 'How about these?'

'Just the thing,' Cass agreed, sitting the baby down

on the pale cord-carpeted floor. She removed the lid from the tube and arranged the balls in front of him. 'All yours.'

Jack batted them with a small hand and set one of the balls shooting away.

'Way to go,' Gifford encouraged, and kicked it back.

The little boy watched as the ball rolled past him, then began to play with the plastic container.

She grinned. 'Typical.'

'Last night you talked about having sent me letters,' Gifford said, crossing to the other side of the kitchen where he plugged in an electric kettle.

'Two,' Cass told him.

He turned to her, muscled arms folded across his chest. A moment ago his manner had been easy, but a tightening in his expression and the gun-metal grey of his eyes warned that his mood had changed.

'You really sent them?' he enquired. 'Or, when you discovered you were pregnant, did you decide not to bother about informing me because that would've complicated matters? Because I'd been merely a stud service?'

She marched over to stand beside him. 'I decided nothing of the sort!'

'These days, plenty of young women seem to regard their children's fathers as expendable.' Gifford was keeping his voice low in order not to disturb the baby, yet every word he spoke was cold, hard steel. 'They let the guy impregnate them, then wave goodbye.'

'Not me,' Cass pronounced, her eyes ablaze. 'I consider that children need fathers to give them love and security, and to help them grow into confident, rounded adults. And,' she added, 'I do not lie!'

He subjected her to a piercing assessment, then began to spoon instant-coffee granules into two porcelain beakers. He was, he acknowledged, too suspicious, too cynical—which was doubtless due to his dear old father.

'I believe you,' he said.

'So you damn well should!' she snapped.

'My accusation was unfair and I apologise. I know you have integrity and would never attempt a stunt like that.'

'Thank you,' Cass said, her tone calmer. 'I sent you two letters,' she continued, looking across at the baby who was engrossed in banging the lid against the plastic tube. 'One saying I was pregnant and a second advising you of Jack's birth. I gave the first to Stephen to give to you when he was in Boston, and he assured me he'd handed it over.'

'He gave me nothing. You'd told him the contents of the letter?' Gifford enquired.

'No. I felt that that was strictly between the two of us.'

Her brow crinkled. 'Perhaps Stephen lost the letter, then didn't like to own up.'

'I doubt it,' he said curtly. 'My guess is that he'd figured it said something of importance to me and decided not to deliver it. The guy may've resisted the urge to get up a petition to have me shot, but he hates my guts.'

Cass gave a rueful nod. 'Stephen resents the fact that you, as part of Tait-Hill, bought out Dexter's and thus exposed him as inefficient. And that you're personally successful.'

'Plus it riled him when you and I got along so well. Even though he wasn't your boyfriend, he felt he had a claim on you and regarded me as an intruder. Which is why when I spoke to him on the phone he took great delight in telling me that you'd moved in with him.'

'You said you rang to ask about me?'

'I did.' Gifford frowned as he poured hot water into the beakers. 'I felt bad about the way I'd...ended our affair.'

'You were too abrupt?' she suggested.

He nodded. 'But I didn't want you to think we had a future and—' He stopped, as if uncertain about what he had been going to say.

'I didn't think that,' Cass declared, into the silence.

'OK. Anyhow, I rang because I wanted to know how you were getting along. You still take your coffee black?'

'Please. Why didn't you speak to me?' she enquired.

'You were out of the office and, for some reason, the telephonist put me through to Stephen. He indicated that you and he were...partners, and made noises about the two of you starting a family.'

She frowned. 'And you spoke to him last winter, so I was pregnant.'

'Yup. Afterwards I thought of how you'd said the guy was like a kid brother and told myself that he wasn't your type, but relationships can change and by dropping his earlier hints Stephen had seemed to indicate he was interested in you, so—' He broke off as Jack let out a sudden squeal. 'What's up, ragtag?'

The plastic tube had rolled away, and the baby was stretching forward in an attempt to retrieve it. But a leg which was tucked beneath him stopped his progress. Sitting upright, Jack stretched his arms out wide, clenched his fists and filled his lungs. 'Yaaah!' He let out a screech which would have awakened the dead.

Cass walked over, giving him the tube and rounding up the tennis balls. 'He's desperate to crawl, but he can't work out how to do it. He gets so frustrated.'

'I know the feeling,' Gifford said brusquely. He carried their coffees to the pine breakfast bar which curved

out into the room. 'When did you send the second letter?'

'In March, when Jack was a month old.'

'March was when I had my accident,' he said, pulling
a chair out from beneath the bar and sitting down. 'You
mailed it to my apartment?'

'No.' She sat alongside him. 'I don't have your home
address, so I sent it to your office.'

'My secretary probably included the letter in a stack
of get-well cards which she brought out to the hospital.'
He cast her a look. 'I got so tired of receiving cards
which had bright-eyed cartoon characters spouting en-
couraging ''perk up'' messages that before long I started
dumping them. Unopened. I know I shouldn't have done,
because folk were being kind, but—'

'You were feeling sorry for yourself?'

'I guess,' he said, and she saw something in his face
which spoke of past pain, resignation and general world-
weariness. He turned to look at the baby who was en-
deavouring to chew the tennis-ball tube. 'When I didn't
answer your letters, you ought to have phoned me.'

Cass nodded. 'I did think about ringing several times,
and once I got as far as dialling your office number,
but—'

'But what?' Gifford enquired, when she hesitated.

'I was damned if I'd chase you up and be regarded
as a pest.' Her chin lifted. 'I refused to play the victim.'

He gave a dry smile. 'There's never been any danger
of that,' he said, and they fell silent, drinking their coffee
and watching the baby.

His failure to answer her letters would have seemed
a logical progression from him so abruptly terminating
their relationship, Gifford reflected. But he had realised
he was falling in love, had found himself wondering
about marriage—and been gripped by a desperate urge

to escape. He frowned. His experience of marriage—which meant his father's marriages—had had a searing effect.

'Jack looks like me,' he said.

'I wondered whether when you saw him you'd see the resemblance—and you did.'

'Yes, though I had a hard time getting my mind around it. Last night, I was surprised that he didn't look anything at all like Stephen, and then—when you told me how old he was—it dawned that I must be his father.' Gifford shook a wondering head. 'It was such a shock that it took me a while to believe it.'

'Discovering I was pregnant shocked me, too,' Cass said wryly.

'I can imagine.' His grey eyes met hers. 'But do you know when it happened?'

'On the morning you left to go back to the States.'

'When you stripped off your clothes and came into the shower.' His gaze locked onto hers. 'You asked me to make love to you, and I was in such a damn rush to oblige that I entered you without—'

'We made a mistake,' she said, cutting him off.

She had enough trouble with her own recollections without him taking them on an erotic trip down memory lane.

'When you realised you were pregnant, you didn't consider…termination?' Gifford enquired.

'No, though when you failed to answer my first letter I wondered if you hadn't replied because you hoped your silence might steer me in that direction.'

'I'd never attempt to "steer" something like that,' he protested, his tone offended. 'But you didn't want to settle down. "Not yet. Not for a long time",' he quoted, showing a surprising recall of the previous year's conversation.

'I changed my mind. A woman's prerogative,' Cass said lightly.

Although she had been happy as a career girl and had spoken the truth at the time, she had not, for one moment, regretted having Jack—even if his appearance had turned her life upside down.

'I want to help you financially,' Gifford told her.

She had anticipated his offer and had fixed her response.

'Thanks, and I'll accept maintenance for Jack. But I don't want anything for me.'

'You've given up your job to look after him,' he said, with a crackle of impatience. 'And this bed and breakfast scheme may not bring in much.'

'I'll manage.'

'Why "manage" when I have ample cash? I can easily—'

'No!'

His grey eyes flashed. 'Do you have to be so bloody obstinate?'

'I want to be as independent as I can. It's important to me,' Cass insisted.

'You don't feel inclined to be a kept woman?'

'No, thanks.'

Gifford spread his hands in an 'I give up' gesture. 'Your choice. I've no idea how much it costs to feed and clothe a child, so suppose I arrange for five thousand dollars a month to be paid into your bank account? Backdated to the date of Jack's birth.'

'That's far too much,' she protested.

'I can afford it, and it's important to *me*,' he said, in an iron-clad tit-for-tat.

Cass sighed. 'I'll work out my monthly budget and we can discuss it again.'

'OK.' He finished his coffee. 'You said you hadn't

had an affair with Stephen; does that mean you've never been intimate with him?'

'It does.'

'When you first told me you had a baby I decided that the two of you must've had a one-night stand.'

'That I needed solace because I was on the rebound from you?' she suggested.

Gifford frowned. Although her response to his ending of their affair had been casual, he had always wondered if she might have been acting. But perhaps he hoped she had acted, and was deceiving himself?

'Something like that,' he said.

'No. And,' Cass added, 'I don't go in for one-night stands.'

'It seemed out of character—and, for the record, neither do I. Has Stephen never come on to you?' he went on.

She shook her head. 'Like you said he isn't my type, and—' her brow creased '—I'm not his type, either.'

'Yet he suggested you should move into his apartment?'

'Yes, but although he was helping me Stephen was also helping himself. You see, for years his father's been attempting to marry him off to the daughter of a neighbour who's a high-ranking judge,' she began to explain. 'Henry's a snob and the connection appeals. He's invited the daughter to umpteen Dexter family dinners and done his damnedest to throw the two of them together, but Stephen isn't interested.'

'Have you met the girl?' Gifford enquired.

'Once, when she came to collect Stephen from the office and take him to a party. She seemed pleasant, if a little colourless. But having me living in his apartment gave him the excuse to hint at an alternative relationship.

And if he hinted I was having his child that would really have got her—and his father—off his back.'

'So you reckon he dropped hints to other people as well as to me?'

Cass nodded. 'Men and women are often flatmates, pure and simple, and when I moved into his apartment I assumed everyone would see the arrangement that way. After all, I paid rent and had my own room, and a separate social life. But, as time went by, people at the office began to drop the odd comment which made me wonder what Stephen was saying. At the time, I dismissed them, but now—' She sighed. 'I suspect he could've been spreading the rumour that Jack was his, but asking whoever he told to keep it confidential.'

'No one ever said anything outright to you?'

'It was just vague innuendo.'

'Doesn't the guy have a proper girlfriend?'

'He's never had one in all the time I've known him.'

Gifford shot her a look. 'Does he travel on the other bus? Is he gay?'

'I think he could be,' she admitted. 'Though, if so, he's still firmly in the closet.'

'Because he's frightened of his father's reaction?'

'Yes. And Stephen wanting to conceal any gay tendency could have been another reason for him installing me in his apartment et cetera.'

He frowned. 'If he does leave the firm and gets away from Henry's influence, it'd be a damn good thing.'

'I agree. Stephen needs to grow up and be his own person. He—'

She stopped. Jack had coughed. As she swung to look at him, the baby went red in the face and coughed again. It was a tight, straining sound.

'He's swallowed something,' she declared, diving

from her chair to kneel beside him. 'Oh, heavens, he's choking!'

Wanting to hook out whatever it was he had in his mouth, she pushed a finger between his lips. The baby spluttered, heaved and reared away. He coughed again. She raised her hand to his mouth a second time, but he jammed his lips tight together.

'Please, Jack, *please*,' she implored in desperation, but he fended her off.

As she gave a helpless wail of dismay, Gifford rose, bent over and tapped the child sharply on the back.

'Cough it up,' he instructed. Jack coughed, and a small disc of soggy white paper, which was part of the label, flew out of his mouth and landed on the carpet. 'Good kid,' he said.

Pulling the baby to her, Cass held him close. 'Oh, Giff, thank you, thank you,' she said, babbling in her relief. 'I thought he was going to choke to death, and—'

'You panicked.'

'Yes.' With Jack in her arms, she clambered to her feet. 'I'm pretty cool in most circumstances, but when it comes to him I—'

'Mothers always worry themselves sick about their kids. It's human nature.' He tickled the baby under his chin. 'You had your dad worried for a moment there, too, so no more gobbling down labels—understand?'

When Jack giggled, Cass felt a sudden, heartwarming awareness of them as a threesome—parents with their child.

Reaching out, she took hold of Gifford's hand. 'Thanks for coming to the rescue.'

He raised her fingers to his lips. 'Any time,' he said, and kissed them.

Her heartbeat accelerated. The touch of his mouth on

her skin and the look in his grey eyes had set her pulses stirring.

Withdrawing her hand, Cass inspected her watch. 'Time's rolling on,' she said, with a chirpy smile. 'Thanks for the coffee and for delivering this one from the jaws of death—' she nuzzled into Jack's neck, making him giggle again '—but now I must go and waitress for the tour party.'

'Do you have the phone number of a taxi firm?' Gifford enquired as he walked with her along the hall. 'I need to shop for food, and I'd also like to buy some typing paper.'

'So you can work on your idiot's guide?'

'Right. I'm a two-finger typist, but my writing's close to illegible. If you recall, I have difficulty reading it myself at times.'

She swung him a smile. 'I do. There's a taxi number back at the restaurant. But haven't you thought about hiring a car while you're here?'

'I intended to,' he told her, 'but the company could only provide a manual, and my busted leg means I'm unable to drive one.'

Cass frowned. This was a drawback to his injury which had not occurred to her and, she realised, there must be others.

'I'm going into Grand Anse to stock up on groceries this afternoon, so I could take you,' she offered. 'I'll be leaving when the tour party departs at around two, so that I'm back in time to meet Kirk Weber at five-fifteen.'

Gifford nodded. 'Thanks. I'll come over.'

'Thank you for offering to pay for Jack's upkeep.' She hesitated, choosing her words. 'Are you happy to be a father to him as he grows up? Will you visit him and play a role in his life?'

A shutter seemed to roll down his face, closing off his emotions and holding her away.

'It's not a good idea,' he said.

Puzzled, she frowned. His introduction to Jack had seemed to go so well. 'But you like him?'

'Yes.'

'Taking him on the occasional holiday wouldn't tie you down. OK, you living on one side of the Atlantic and Jack living on the other is a little tricky, but—'

'It wouldn't work,' Gifford broke in curtly. 'It's not the best thing for him.'

'Why not?'

'Because—' He shook his head. 'No.'

'The idea of looking after a child doesn't fit into your agenda? But it'll only be once in a while, and—'

'Drop it,' he rasped.

Cass blinked back the hot sting of tears. Perhaps the odds had always been stacked against him—the man who needed his freedom—taking an ongoing interest in their son. But to hear him disown that interest—damn near disown Jack—created a tidal wave of misery inside her.

Hugging the baby to her, she shone him a smile as brittle as glass. 'Your choice,' she said.

CHAPTER FIVE

GIFFORD wedged the last bulging shopping bag in amongst the others which crammed the back of the car, then levered his long body down into the seat beside her. He slammed shut the door.

'Just in time,' he said as a fat droplet of rain splashed onto the windscreen.

Cass nodded. 'It looks like we might be in for a storm.'

The weather forecast had warned that November's north-west monsoon could bring erratic squalls, and an hour ago, when they had parked on Grand Anse's sleepy main street, clouds had been building on the horizon. As they had made their way from the newsagent's shop to colourful fruit and vegetable stalls and then to the well-stocked mini-market, a breeze had sprung up and the clouds had rolled in closer. Now they hung overhead, making a low ceiling of ominous grey.

'Is this thing waterproof?' he enquired, shooting a doubtful look around.

They were in her uncle's ancient Mini Moke which had rusting yellow bodywork, a mildewed canvas roof and a no-frills interior. The roll-down canvas sides were secured to the body by metal studs, but some of the studs were broken and the canvas had a tendency to gape.

'No idea; I've never driven it in the rain,' she replied, and pulled away from the kerb. 'But with luck we should be back before it gets too heavy.'

'Does Jack like travelling in cars?' Gifford asked, glancing back at the baby seat.

There was so much about his son—*his son, their son*;
the words inspired a whole tangle of feelings—which he
did not know. His hand tightened around the walking
stick which he had accommodated between his knees.
And so much which he was destined not to know.

'He loves it,' Cass said, her mind going to the child,
whom, because he had been asleep, Edith had insisted
they should leave with her. 'He loves going over bumps,
so he thinks being driven around the island in the Moke
is bliss.'

She smiled as she spoke and kept her tone bright.
Although earlier his refusal to play an active part in the
little boy's life had seemed a major catastrophe, she had
managed to recover her composure. She had strength,
will and resilience. She did not fold easily. She *would*
not fold.

After all, she had rationalised, the situation with
Gifford was pretty much what she had believed it to be
at the start of the week, so it was back to square one.
Nothing had changed. She darted him a look. Nor could
she change anything; his flat refusal to even talk about
the subject had made that brutally clear.

'Damn,' Cass muttered, switching on the wipers as a
fat droplet was joined by another and another.

Within minutes, the rain was thrumming in a relent-
less rhythm on the roof and bouncing off the bonnet. It
was of the heavy, tropical, stair-rod variety.

She frowned out at the narrow road. In Grand Anse
the metalled surface had been in good repair, but as the
small community had been left behind and a turn at a
junction had swung them alongside the ocean the tarmac
had petered out into stony red earth and potholes had
begun to appear. Some were small, while others had
more in common with the Grand Canyon.

'Slow down,' Gifford said, when, in avoiding one

hole, she swept dangerously close to another. 'Who do you think you are—a Formula One racing driver?'

She surreptitiously braked—her speed had been a touch fast and the road did resemble a tank range—then glanced out sideways through the crumpled plastic window. Ever since her arrival on the island, the sea had been a placid turquoise blue, but today it heaved in turbulent charcoal-grey. White-topped waves surged and crashed on the shore. The breeze had stiffened into a wind, which was billowing through the undergrowth and bending the coconut palms.

As a sudden gust buffeted the Moke, she tightened her grip on the wheel.

'Drop down a gear,' he instructed.

Cass hesitated, then thrust rebelliously, and gratingly, into third.

'I wonder why it is that when it comes to driving men always seem to think they know better than women?' she asked, her tone sweetly acidic.

He gave a smile which was very confident, very male. 'Because they do?'

Before she could retaliate, the wind swooped again. It snatched at the sides of the Moke, broke their tenuous hold on the studs and sent the canvas wildly flapping. The rain lashed in, spattering on their faces and showering their clothes.

Gifford cursed. He reached out a hand, caught hold of the canvas beside him and held it down. Now he was protected. Following his example, Cass made a desperate lunge and managed to grab her side.

'Gotcha!' she crowed, triumphantly yanking down the canvas.

He frowned. 'Driving one-handed isn't wise. All it needs is another gust like that one and you could find yourself careering across the road, down through the bushes and onto the sand. Even into the sea.'

Her chin jutted. Her temper flared. 'Thanks for alerting me to the possibilities, but I'm perfectly safe,' she informed him loftily. 'In the ten years since I passed my driving test I have never been given a parking ticket, let alone crashed a car. Whereas you— Good grief!'

Another high-velocity blast hit, knocking the Moke into a sideways slither. Cass pulled frantically at the wheel in an attempt to regain control, but a moment later the front wheels bucked down into a water-logged pothole, the engine cut out and the vehicle stopped dead in a jolting shudder of bodywork.

In the silence which followed, Gifford lifted a brow. 'Perfectly safe?' he enquired.

She ignored him. She fired the ignition and pressed her foot down on the accelerator, but although the wheels spun round the Moke failed to move. A second later, the engine cut out. She switched off and tried again. Same response.

'You don't imagine you can simply drive out of here?' he asked, when her third attempt proved unlucky.

Cass glared. A couple of days ago, she had thought she could not hate him, but at this moment she did. She hated him because he was so calmly know-all...and because he had rejected Jack.

'What would you suggest?' she enquired, flinging the words at him like small bricks.

'That we push the Moke out of the hole and onto the level.'

'Push? But it's pouring down.'

'And the longer it rains, the deeper the water in the hole will become and the more difficult it'll be to get free,' Gifford said, the soul of reason. He tapped out a casual rhythm on a denim-clad knee. 'But perhaps you have a better solution?'

Her teeth ground together. 'No.'

'Then if you stand at your side and guide the steering wheel I'll heave from the back.' Reaching over in amongst the shopping, he located a brightly coloured golf umbrella which had belonged to her uncle. 'Some spokes are broken, but this should give you cover. Put the car out of gear and leave the handbrake off.'

'Already done,' Cass said. 'I'm not totally stupid.'

'You have a certificate to that effect?' he asked, and got out.

Opening her door, she put up the brolly—which was not an easy operation in the wind and driving rain. When she climbed onto the road, she found that Gifford had positioned himself with two hands on the rear of the Moke.

'Shouldn't have much trouble,' he said, experimentally rocking the vehicle forward and back. He swiped spears of dark wet hair out of his eyes. 'I'll count to three and then I'll push.'

She nodded and, reaching in through her door, took hold of the wheel. Wedging the handle of the umbrella carefully beneath her arm, Cass prepared to push with her other hand. No matter how infuriating he was, by rescuing them her companion was being the gallant knight, and so she must help. His gallantry meant him standing out in the rain and, although neither of them had mentioned it, him running the risk of putting a strain on his leg.

'One. Two. *Three,*' he said, and heaved.

The front wheels jerked up over the jagged edge and the Moke started to roll forward. Cass was giving mental thanks when the rear wheels galumphed briefly into the pothole before moving out, water shot up in a perfect arc—and fell on her.

'Ugh!'

The water was muddy and surprisingly cold. It drenched her hair and soused down her dress, transforming it into a soggy rag. She was standing beneath the umbrella, yet she had been soaked. It was not fair!

'Dear me,' Gifford said.

Blinking behind a curtain of dripping rat's tails, she turned to see that he had stepped back and so had escaped. Clever devil, she thought furiously, then she noticed that his mouth was twitching.

'It isn't funny!' she protested.

'Indeed not,' he agreed, though he was having difficulty schooling his expression.

Cass hooked the rat's tails out of her eyes. Light brown rivulets were streaming down her face, her bare shoulders, and soaking into her bodice. The skirt of her dress stuck clammily to her legs and when she moved her feet her sandals squelched.

'Ever thought of mud wrestling as a profession?' Gifford enquired.

She dashed a trickle of water from her chin. 'Not recently.'

'Maybe you should consider it instead of doing bed and breakfasts.'

The look which she flung him would have roasted an ox. 'Maybe you should can the quips!'

'Yes, ma'am,' he replied, grinning, and, walking forward, he reached into the Moke to fix the handbrake. As he straightened up, his amusement faded. 'Is it go-as-bare-as-you-dare week?'

'Excuse me?'

'You might want to wear a bra the next time you wear that dress,' he said, his voice abruptly curt.

Cass glanced down. Because her strapless bra dated from pre-baby days and was on the tight side, she had left it off that morning. The printed cotton of her sundress gave respectable cover—or it had when it was dry. But, soaked with water, the material had become semisheer. It clung to the high curves of her breasts like a second skin, revealing tantalising shadows of honey-brown aureoles and—because the splash of water had been cold—the jut of her nipples.

As heat filled her cheeks, she darted him a look. The rain had wet his shirt and plastered it to the wall of his chest, while his dampened jeans clung to his thighs. His dark hair was tousled. All of a sudden, she was overwhelmingly aware of him as a raunchy, powerful male and aware of herself as a provocative, shapely female. Gifford's terse manner said that he was aware of it, too.

'If you get inside I'll fix the studs,' he told her, and as she climbed back into the driving seat he made his way systematically around the Moke, refastening the canvas.

'Roll the wagon,' he instructed, when he returned to sit inside.

Cass started the engine and they moved forward—and kept on moving. 'How did you come to crash your car?' she enquired, driving more cautiously now and keeping well clear of the potholes. 'Did you swerve to avoid an animal or—?'

'I swerved to avoid Imogen Sales having her wicked way with me,' he said abrasively.

'Which means?'

'She made a sexual suggestion and put her hand on my thigh. I pushed it away, she returned her fingers, and in fighting her off I lost concentration for a second and consequently control of the car.'

She slid him a look. 'You felt it was the wrong time and place?'

'It'd never been the right time or place with her. I told you the relationship was brief; that was because I quickly realised Imogen was attempting to use me—' a muscle tightened in his jaw '—and because I didn't much like the woman.'

'So why go out with her?' Cass enquired. She recalled the trade journal quote. 'Why become "an item"?'

'I didn't say that, Imogen did, out of my hearing. And she lied, because we weren't a couple—then or ever. The photograph gave the wrong impression. We'd only just been introduced when a guy with a camera appeared and—' Gifford raised his brows '—what do you know?—she's hugging me.'

'You were taken by surprise?'

'Completely, and I was surprised when she suggested we should have dinner together the following evening. I'm aware that in these enlightened times it's entirely acceptable for women to make the running, but Imogen was so damned insistent.'

'And you were flattered?'

'Not so much flattered as—' His expression sombre, he stared at the road ahead. 'I felt in need of a diversion, so I agreed. We went out a couple of times, at her suggestion, but whatever I talked about she invariably steered the conversation around to who did I know in the television industry? If I was invited to TV parties, would I take her along? Could I fix a meeting for her with this studio boss or that director?'

'She was hoping you'd help her career?'

'It was the only reason she'd latched onto me,' Gifford said grimly.

'Imogen must've fancied you, too. Come on, you're—' On the brink of describing him in glowing terms—words like smart, charismatic and sexy had sprung to mind—Cass broke off. She was damned if she would praise him. 'Imogen must've fancied you,' she repeated.

'A little, perhaps,' he conceded, 'but her career came first. She wasn't climbing the ladder of stardom as rapidly as she felt she should, and she believed my connections might assist. Also she hoped that being connected with me, being seen with me, would drum up some publicity.'

'Which it did, because the photo of the two of you appeared in the trade journal.'

'The photo appeared in a couple of mainstream magazines, too, together with the ''item'' quote. So she got some play out of it,' Gifford said, and scowled.

'Did you fix any meetings for her?' Cass enquired.

'None. I believe in people making it on their own merits, plus I object to being used. I explained all that and said it was farewell. At which point Imogen played the drama queen—badly. She moved from grand outrage to hand-wringing to lying seductively down on the sofa, and when I remained unimpressed she flounced off.'

Cass switched off the windscreen wipers. The storm was over. The rain had stopped, the wind had died and the clouds were edging away to reveal ribbons of blue. Pale sunlight shimmered over the sea.

'If you only went out a couple of times, why was Imogen with you in your car?' she questioned.

'Because one morning, after months had gone by, and when I was on the point of leaving for a business appointment, she walked into my office. I'd been sure I was rid of the bloody woman, but—' Gifford expelled an impatient breath '—I was wrong.'

'What did she want?'

'Apparently a TV guy whom I vaguely knew was

casting for a soap opera and she'd auditioned, but he'd turned her down. Imogen vowed that if I had a word with him he would change his mind. I told her she was mistaken, that, in any case, I wasn't willing to speak to anyone on her behalf, and said, Sorry, I must go. However, when I went down to the parking lot she followed and climbed into my car. I asked her to get out, but she refused.'

Cass raised a brow. 'You just asked her?'

'I asked her. There were other people around and I didn't want to cause a scene by throwing her out—which is what she deserved. By this time I was running late,' he continued, 'so I set off. It was a one-hour drive—'

'Did Imogen know that?' she cut in.

'Yup. For the first few miles I kept expecting her to demand that I stop and let her out, but she must've decided that sixty minutes of drip-drip-drip would wear me down. On the journey there I ignored her, and I hoped that when I disappeared to keep my appointment she'd give up and disappear, too. She could've gotten a train back,' he explained. 'But, when I returned to my car, she was waiting.'

'You were furious?'

'And how! Damn near jumped up and down in a tantrum. My one aim was to offload the woman as quickly as possible, so I went way over the speed limit on the drive back to Boston. After trying every kind of verbal appeal to persuade me to speak to the soap opera guy, Imogen started on sexual inducements.' Gifford made a face. 'She offered to perform a service which, I understand, is more usually offered to rock stars in the back of stretch limos. When I said no, thanks, she endeavoured to have her way—and we skidded.'

Cass slowed, turning off the road and onto the gravelled drive which led down to Maison d'Horizon. Now the sun shone in a clear blue sky. The wet-sleeked leaves of palm trees gleamed and raindrops sparkled amongst the greenery. Steam rose. The sweet smell of freshly washed earth filled the air.

'Imogen must've felt dreadful about the accident—dreadful about being to blame for what happened to you,' she said.

He shook his head. 'She came to the hospital and apologised, but all she was really bothered about was her career. She begged me not to tell anyone the reason why we'd crashed. Any publicity is reckoned to be better than no publicity, but even she could see that if I revealed the truth it wasn't going to put her in a good light,' Gifford said sardonically. 'Once I'd agreed, she shot off, and I haven't heard from her since.'

'She didn't keep a check on your progress?'

'Nope.'

'The bitch!'

He smiled at the ferocity of her protest. 'She was. She is. Thanks for acting as chauffeur,' he said as Cass drew the Moke to a halt outside his front door. 'I'll unload my stuff.'

She climbed out. 'I'll help.'

'You don't think it'd be a good idea to cover yourself up?' he enquired as she carried bags into the kitchen.

She glanced down. The wet dress still clung, outlining the curve of her breasts and their brazenly pointed nipples. She looked like a torrid vamp in some Italian movie, Cass thought—and her companion had become terse again.

'I'm bothering you?' she asked, her tone flippant.

Whilst she needed to fight an urge to cross her hands demurely over her chest, to be unsettling him seemed a sweet revenge. Gifford had been attempting to ignore her appearance, but his body language—a tightness around his mouth, a tension in the set of his shoulders—indicated he was all too aware of it.

'A little,' he bit out.

'I have no idea why. After all, you've seen me naked. Completely naked.'

'A long time ago,' he rasped. Grim-faced, he dumped his load and reached for a towel. 'Here.'

She dried the worst of the wet from her hair, then laid the towel down. Gifford had expected her to drape it over herself, but she refused to oblige. She refused to fall in with his wishes when he would not fall in with hers—about Jack.

'Are you intending to change before your meeting with Kirk Weber?' he enquired, as a give-away nerve pulsed in his temple.

'Of course,' Cass replied, with a blithe smile, then she hesitated. 'Would you be willing to sit in on the meeting? Not to say anything—unless you wanted to—but to be a male presence. Having you there might make him think twice about attempting any more tricks, and—and I'd be grateful.'

'Let's do a deal. You cover your goddamn breasts,' Gifford said grittily, 'and I'll act as observer.'

'Done,' she agreed, and, placing the towel around her shoulders, she drew it respectably down.

He gave a curt nod of approval. 'I'll get out of my wet clothes and come straight round.'

'I'll wait and take you in the Moke.'

'You figure that if I walk I might fall?' he demanded.

Although he had not mentioned his injured leg when he had pushed the Moke, he was thinking about it now. She knew he was thinking that she was treating him like an invalid—and his hackles had risen.

She looked levelly back. 'It's possible,' she said. 'The

path's steep and will be wet after the rain, so anyone could go sprawling.'

A beat went by. 'Give me five minutes,' he said.

When they arrived at the Forgotten Eden, the silver Toyota saloon which Veronica hired was parked in the yard. Together they unloaded the other bags of groceries and then went through to the restaurant. The redhead, who wore a turquoise shift dress, was cooing over Jack who sat on her lap, while Edith folded napkins at a table beside them.

'What's happened to you?' Edith enquired, looking at Cass in surprise, and Cass explained how she had been drenched.

'Has Jack been OK?' she asked as she completed her story.

'He's been hunky-dory,' Edith assured her.

'Not missed you at all,' Veronica declared. 'We've had such fun. We've been playing "Ride a Cock horse" all afternoon.' She bounced him up and down on her knee in demonstration. 'Haven't we, my precious?'

Raising his eyes to Cass, the baby gave her a weary look.

'Veronica arrived a few minutes after you left,' said Edith, who seemed a mite jaded, too.

'I wanted to get away from Club Sesel and all the moaning,' the redhead declared. 'People were moaning about the storm and what a mess it'll have made of the road, and they were complaining about the swimming.'

'What about the swimming?' Gifford enquired.

'It isn't mentioned in the brochure, but the pool's tiny, and the sea at the hotel is shallow and clogged with weed, so anyone who wants to swim has no place to go. It's a constant grumble.'

'How about you coming to me?' Cass said, eager to rescue Jack from Veronica's grasp.

She bent to lift the baby, but the redhead cuddled him closer. 'I'm happy with him. I wish I had a lovely baby boy like you, don't I, my precious?' she crooned, pressing her cheek against his.

As Jack squirmed, Gifford stepped forward. 'He'd be happier with his mother,' he said, in a granite-edged voice.

Veronica pouted coyly. 'Spoilsport,' she said, and handed the baby over.

Jack was resting thankfully against Cass when the telephone rang on the bar. Edith went to answer it.

'Jules won't be here until this evening,' she reported as she replaced the receiver. 'He was planning to come in early, around now, to check the stocks—like I told you,' she said to Veronica. 'But he can't make it.'

The visitor pouted again. 'Then I shall go.' Rising, she said goodbye, and then smiled longingly at Jack. 'I'll see you again.'

'Veronica was due to fly home this weekend, but she's decided to extend her holiday by another ten days,' Edith revealed, when the redhead had gone. 'What d'you bet she spends most of those days here?' She sighed and turned towards the kitchen. 'I'll make a start on dinner preparations before Kirk arrives.'

'I asked Gifford if he'd sit in on the meeting and he's agreed,' Cass said. 'You don't mind?'

'I think it's a great idea,' the older woman declared, and beamed at him. 'Thanks.'

He grinned. 'Hope my presence helps.'

'Another ten days of Veronica—poor Jules,' Cass said as Edith disappeared.

'And poor Jack.' Gifford frowned. 'When you attempted to take him off her she looked ready to start a tug-of-war.' He stroked the baby's hand with a gentle finger. 'Not nice, was it, ragtag?'

Jack smiled at him and gurgled.

'I realise it could be difficult,' he went on, 'but over these next ten days try and keep Veronica away from him.'

Cass bristled. The disinterested father was giving his orders—how dared he?

'Are you telling me how to look after Jack?' she enquired, her voice glacial.

'I'm suggesting you keep Veronica clear of him,' he said levelly. 'You might feel sorry for the woman, but I don't trust her. She's too excitable.' He cast a glance towards the swing doors. 'Does Edith know that I'm Jack's father?'

'No one knows, only my family. You look worn out,' she said, when the baby opened his mouth into a perfect oval and gave a long, long yawn. 'If I lay you down in your buggy will you go to sleep?'

'I'll put him in his buggy and wheel him around while you get changed,' Gifford said, and held out his hands.

After a moment's hesitation, she passed Jack over. 'Go ahead.'

Kirk Weber was not due to arrive for over an hour so, after stripping off her muddy clothes, Cass showered and shampooed her hair. Wrapping a cream-coloured bath towel around her, she walked into her bedroom and plugged in the hair-drier. Gifford's offer to take care of the baby had surprised her, she thought as she untangled her long blonde tresses. And when he had offered she had been tempted to say that if he didn't wish to be involved as the little boy grew up he must have nothing to do with him now. But Jack had been leaning towards him. The traitor... The innocent...

When her hair was dry, Cass took a silky lemon top from a hanger in the lopsided rattan wardrobe. The top would be teamed with short white leggings, but where were the leggings? Crossing to a chest of drawers, she began to root through.

'You're searching for a bra?' a deep voice enquired, and she glanced back to find Gifford standing in the doorway with one broad shoulder resting against the frame. His eyes went to the white lace bra and matching panties which she had laid out on the bed. 'You've found one. Thank the Lord.'

She straightened. She might have entered his villa and watched him shaving, but she did not appreciate him walking into the cottage and watching her.

'Don't you know how to ring a bell?' she demanded. 'One, you poke out your finger and, two, you push. Like this!'

Swinging round to face him, Cass jabbed a finger, but as she swivelled the towel which had been tucked in beneath her armpits came adrift. It fell, slithering first to her waist and, a millisecond later, dropping down to form a soft, creamy puddle at her feet.

She was hastily bending to retrieve the towel when he stepped forward, put his hands on her shoulders and held her upright.

'I did poke and push,' Gifford said, 'but when I rang the bell there was no answer. And when I listened I heard a distant hum.'

'I was drying my hair.'

'So you didn't hear me.' He frowned. 'Are you doing this on purpose?'

'Do—doing what?' Cass faltered, woefully aware of being naked with him and in a bedroom. It was a disturbing reminder of the past.

'Trying to arouse me.' His mouth twisted into an ironic smile. 'Congratulations—you're being successful.'

'The towel fell off by accident.'

'Is that right?'

'Yes, it is! And I would like to put on some clothes,' she declared, intending to issue a demand, but hearing her words sound more like a plea.

If he was aroused, so was she. Shamefully, recklessly, wildly so. If he should decide to pull her down with him onto the bed and make violent love, it seemed doubtful she would find the strength to resist.

'There's no hurry,' he said, his hands firm on her shoulders. 'Like you said earlier, I've seen you naked before. And as it was a long time ago I need to refresh my memory.' His grey eyes trailed down, scanning her figure with a lazily insolent thoroughness. 'You're more womanly,' he said. 'I like it.'

'And I would like to put on some clothes,' Cass repeated, in a voice which had become unconsciously husky.

Dropping his arms, he stood back. By touching her, by looking at her silken nudity, by remembering how it had been when he had buried his body in hers, he was torturing himself.

'I'll wait in the living room,' Gifford said, and strode out, pulling the door almost closed behind him.

She released a thankful sigh. 'Why are you here?' she called as she swiftly fastened on her bra and stepped into her briefs.

'I came to tell you that Jack is asleep and Kirk Weber has arrived.'

She consulted her watch. It was a quarter to five. She drew on the lemon top and found the leggings.

'Kirk's here already?' she protested, opening the door and looking out.

She was dressed; all she had to do now was comb her hair, apply a dash of lip gloss and fix in her gold hoop earrings.

'He said he'd got away early.' Hooking his thumbs into the hip pockets of his jeans, Gifford frowned. 'Early from what? Does the guy have other business deals going on on the island?'

'Not so far as I know.'

'Anyway the cool dude's waiting, drenched in cologne and decked out in his designer suit.'

'Is it silver-grey gabardine?' Cass asked.

He looked through to where she was standing in front of a mirror, colouring her lips. When they had been together in the past he had enjoyed watching her attend to such personal female requirements, and he was enjoying it now.

'Yes,' he said. 'Why?'

'Because when I was at Club Sesel the other day I saw a man in a grey gabardine suit and I wondered if it could be Kirk,' she said, and explained how she had been at the hair salon. 'He was leaving the manager's office, but he suddenly turned and went back in.'

'To avoid meeting you?'

'It could've been.'

Gifford rubbed a hand pensively along the side of his jaw. 'I wonder if the guy's connected with the hotel? With the management. That would explain why he's always so formally dressed. But in that case why would he want to buy the Forgotten Eden?'

Clipping the golden hoops into her ears, Cass walked towards him. Her brain was buzzing, inspiration surging as she thought back to Veronica's talk of grumbles.

'Because it would give access to the cove?' she suggested.

He nodded. 'The water's deep, and you said it was the only deep place on this stretch of coast. If Club Sesel's guests are complaining amongst themselves about the lack of sea swimming, chances are they'll complain to their travel companies when they get back home.'

'And pass the word around their friends that the place is a no-no.'

'Was the hotel busy when you were there?' he enquired.

'Deathly quiet, and, according to Jules, who's friendly with the waitresses, there are always empty bungalows.'

Gifford grinned. 'So if the place is to remain viable Kirk needs the cove. Needs as in must have at any price.'

'But we don't know for certain that he is connected with the hotel,' she demurred.

Leaning on his cane, he went to open the cottage door. 'Let's go and find out.'

His smile cheesily in place, Kirk Weber was making small talk with Edith in the restaurant. He looked smug, as though their acceptance of his 'half price' ultimatum were already in the bag.

Cass greeted him, went over to check that Jack was still sleeping soundly behind the rattan screen, and returned to find that Gifford had introduced himself.

'Edith and Cass have asked me to sit in on your discussion,' he explained.

As they sat down at the table, the South African tweaked at his shirt collar. Whilst he knew nothing about the younger man, he had recognised an alertness in his grey eyes which warned that his presence should not be taken too lightly.

'Where do you come from?' Kirk enquired, his smile taking on a wary quality.

'He's renting Maison d'Horizon, the house next door,' Edith said, before Gifford could reply. 'He's let us borrow the water glasses, two dozen of them, and he's agreed that Cass can work out on his exercise machines, and—'

'How kind,' the visitor interrupted. He had no patience with an admiring testimonial; all he wanted to do was finalise his purchase. 'And what's your reply to the offer which I made yesterday?'

'The reply is no,' Cass said. 'Half price is not acceptable. So if you wish to withdraw…?'

'I don't,' he shot back, and frowned as if realising he had spoken too quickly.

'Then we've returned to the full price,' she told him.

Kirk tugged at an earlobe. It was clear that paying the full price did not appeal and he was going to offer a less stringent reduction, but wondering at what level.

The white smile shone. 'Sorry, I can't—'

'I'll pay the full price, plus ten per cent,' Gifford said.

Kirk's head whipped round and his eyes seemed to stand out on stalks. 'Pardon me?'

'I'm willing to give you the asking price for the Forgotten Eden, plus ten per cent,' he told Cass. 'Interested?'

'Er—' His statement had surprised her as much as it had surprised the South African, but as she looked into his eyes a sparkle of conspiracy passed between them. 'Very interested,' she said, and turned to Edith. 'Yes?'

The older woman nodded.

'You're making a firm offer?' Kirk demanded.

'It's cast iron,' Gifford said. 'Cash on the table.'

Silence. The tide trickled up the shore and seeped down. Out at sea, a fishing pirogue with brown sails was silhouetted on the horizon.

'I'll give the asking price, plus fifteen per cent,' Kirk said.

'Twenty per cent,' Gifford rapped.

'Twenty-five.'

He nodded. 'You have it.'

The visitor blinked, bewildered by the speed of the

transaction. He had arrived expecting to acquire a bargain, not to end up paying more than his original offer.

'Er—right,' he said.

Gifford looked across at Cass. 'Is that satisfactory?'

'So long as Edith has the money in full by this time next week,' she replied.

'She'll have the money, but I'm afraid it could take a little longer than a week,' Kirk said, now awash with desperate apology. 'You see, I have to refer the increased purchase price to…to someone. It's merely a procedure and I can guarantee they'll agree, but the extra twenty-five per cent will need to be transferred. How about payment in full two weeks on Friday?'

'Sounds acceptable to me,' Cass said, and turned again to Edith, who was sitting bemused and round-eyed. 'What do you think?'

She gave a mute nod.

'But I'll have my cash ready and waiting,' Gifford told the South African. 'So if yours doesn't appear, come the stroke of midnight—'

'It'll be here. I'm buying the property,' Kirk declared pugnaciously, and smiled at Edith. 'First thing tomorrow I shall have the lawyers draw up a contract confirming my purchase at the agreed figure. I'd be grateful if you would sign it.' He stole an oblique look at Gifford. 'Immediately, so that no problems can arise.'

Edith nodded again.

'Smart thinking,' Gifford said, and, leaning back in his chair, he linked his hands behind his head. 'A question,' he added as the older man rose to his feet. 'You mentioned needing to refer the purchase—would that be to the board of Club Sesel?'

Kirk stiffened. 'Club Sesel?'

'In buying the Forgotten Eden, you're acting on behalf

of the company which owns the hotel,' he said, and glanced across at Cass. 'You're an employee.'

'I'm a director,' the South African announced.

'And Club Sesel wants this property because they want access to the deep-water cove?' Cass enquired.

Frowning, he shot a snowy white cuff. 'Correct.'

'You'll be closing down the restaurant?' asked Edith, finding her voice at last.

'No. We intend to run it as a more relaxed alternative to the dining room, and to provide drinks and snacks when our guests come along here to bathe.'

'Are you planning to repair the road?' Gifford asked.

Kirk nodded. 'We're liaising with the authorities on that.' Eager to escape, he stepped back. 'I have phone calls to make. Goodbye.'

As he hurried off, Edith gave a rich chuckle and began to laugh. By the time the noise of his Jeep had faded away, she was rocking back and forward in a froth of amusement.

'I didn't—know—what was happening,' she got out, between bouts of laughter. 'But—did you see his face—when Gifford said "plus ten per cent"? He looked like he was about to throw a fit.' She laughed some more, and then she sobered. 'You've sewn him up well and good, and you've got me all that extra money. Thank you,' she said, reaching out to squeeze both their hands. 'Thank you, so much.'

'The purchase isn't guaranteed until the contract has been signed by both parties,' Gifford warned her.

'No, but it won't fall through. I know it,' Edith declared, with conviction, and after offering more grateful thanks she returned happily to the kitchen to continue preparing the dinner.

'It's lucky that Kirk didn't turn right around and say

you could have the Forgotten Eden,' Cass remarked.
'Then you'd have been lumbered.'

'I can think of worse places to buy, and if the guy
should renege—'

'He won't.'

'—I will put my cash on the table.'

She looked at him in surprise. 'Truly?'

'Cross my heart,' he said, and made the apppropriate
gesture.

'What would you do with the property?'

Reaching for his cane, Gifford rose to his feet. 'Close
the restaurant, refurbish the house and cottages, and use
it as a place in the sun for myself, for friends, and Tait-
Hill staff.'

She stood up. 'Thanks for your help with Kirk. Giff,
you were great!' she declared, and reached up and kissed
him.

His mouth was warm and soft and familiar. Cass relaxed against him, but then, abruptly realising the folly
of her action, began to draw away.

His arm came around her waist, preventing her retreat
and pulling her near. 'You're pretty great yourself,' he
murmured, and lowered his head.

His lips parted hers, and as she felt the touch of his
tongue shivers of excitement streaked through her. She
moved closer. She wanted him so much. No, she told
herself, she did not want Gifford. What she craved was
the thrill and the relief of lovemaking. But she was winding an arm around his neck and drowning in his kiss.

He slid his hand beneath her lemon-coloured top and
up to cup her breast, but only for a moment, for need—
a fevered need which took no regard of where they
were—insisted that he wrench up her bra and touch her.
Her skin was smooth, so smooth. He felt the push of her

nipple against his palm—and the greedy stirring of his own body.

All of a sudden, Gifford lifted his mouth from hers. 'Uh-uh,' he said.

Lost in a world of touch and feel and desire, she looked at him. 'What?'

'Our son is crying,' he told her, and, as if to corroborate his statement, a yell sounded from behind the screen.

Cass took a breath, clearing her mind. 'Perfect timing yet again,' she said, and stepped away to swiftly pull her bra back into place and straighten her top.

Gifford frowned. 'I'm beginning to think that his timing sucks,' he muttered, and picked up his cane and limped away.

CHAPTER SIX

FOLDING the small pale blue sleepsuit, Cass placed it on top of the 'done' pile and reached for another. She ironed and folded again. Jack's things took hardly any time, but a washing basket heaped high with her clothes, plus restaurant tablecloths and napkins, awaited her attention. It was Sunday, often a quieter than usual day for customers, and she was in the utility room which opened off from the back of the Forgotten Eden's kitchen, bringing the ironing up to date. Edith, who had stand-by lunch dishes organised, was generally pottering around.

As she worked, Cass thought about Gifford—he seemed to be forever on her mind—and of how, three days ago, she had kissed him. Although the kiss had been inspired by a rush of gratitude, it had been instinctive. More—it had been necessary. A primal need had compelled her to kiss him, to touch him, to be close. Why? Because she remained caught in his spell.

Eighteen months back she had fallen in love with the man and, regardless of how he had casually ditched her and of his refusal now to do his duty and be any kind of a *real* father to Jack, she still loved him. All this time the feeling had been buried, unrecognised—if anyone had hinted at it she would have burst into hoots of incredulous laughter—yet it was true.

Steam hissed as she swept the iron up and down the skirt of her poppy-printed dress. She must be crazy. A masochist. It was pathetic. She ought to think with her head and not with her heart. And she would. She would

118

fall *out* of love, she told herself. It should not be too difficult.

She looked across at Jack who lay flat on his back in the buggy, little arms stretched above his head as he peacefully slept. If she concentrated on Gifford's act of betrayal towards their son, and kept reminding herself what a selfish, uncaring—

But he has his good points, too, insisted a voice inside her head. Plenty. For example, he had helped Edith by bringing Kirk Weber to heel. The day after the upping-the-price meeting, the South African had arrived with a contract to purchase. It had already carried his signature, on behalf of Club Sesel, and Edith had been implored to add hers.

By coincidence, Gifford had been at the Forgotten Eden at the time and, before the older woman signed, Cass had asked him to check the document.

'The deal's above board and definite,' he had assured them.

So now, as she waited to receive the money, Edith was excitedly planning which colour of carpets and curtains she would buy for her new home. They were furnishings which she was only able to afford because she would be getting far more for the Forgotten Eden than anticipated—thanks to Gifford, whom she now treated like a god who had wandered onto earth by mistake.

The last tablecloth pressed, Cass unplugged the iron and folded up the board. Wheeling the pushchair out into the fresh air, she parked it on the verandah beside the kitchen door. Jack's eyes were closed, but the occasional lazy squirm indicated that he would shortly be surfacing from his nap.

'I'm taking my ironing over to the cottage,' she said, passing Edith in the restaurant, 'but I'll be back in a few minutes to prepare Jack's lunch.'

The woman nodded. 'Fine.'

When everything had been put away—the baby's things placed in a chest in his room, the dress hung up in the wardrobe and her tops, shorts et cetera returned to their various drawers—Cass crossed back to the kitchen.

At her request, Edith saved small portions of fresh vegetables and any fruit which were cooked, and Cass now took covered containers from the fridge. Today Jack's menu would be pumpkin and potato with meat gravy, followed by puréed mango for dessert and, finally, a bottle of formula.

When the food was mashed and warmed, she went outside to collect the baby. The pushchair had gone. Leaning over the wooden balustrade, she scanned the yard and peered up along the drive. She had heard no cries, but if Jack was fretful Edith would sometimes wheel him off for a short, pacifying stroll. And the restaurant was empty.

'Edith?' she called, her gaze searching through the palm trees.

'Coming,' a distant voice replied, from inside the house, and a minute or two later the older woman appeared. 'I was upstairs,' she explained.

'Is Jack upstairs, too?'

'No, he's at Maison d'Horizon.'

'With Gifford?' Cass protested, then wondered why she was surprised.

Over the past few days, the newly aware father had taken the baby for walks in his buggy, played with him, or, if he had appeared when he was sleeping, had stood and gazed at him in silence. He might refuse to become involved long-term, yet right now the novelty of having a son seemed to fascinate him.

Cass frowned. Whilst she could not help but feel gratified by his fascination—after all, she thought Jack was pretty fantastic, too—Gifford's visits unsettled her. Every time she saw him, she was conscious of an inner tension. Each time they met she found herself thinking about how good things could have been for the three of them, if only…

'He arrived when you were over in your cottage, saw that Jack was awake and offered to look after him for a while,' Edith told her. 'He was going to wait to ask if that was OK with you, but I told him you wouldn't mind. You don't, do you?'

She hesitated. 'No.'

'Gifford said to give him a ring when you want Jack and he'll bring him straight over.'

'I'll go and get him,' she said.

'Take your time. There are no reservations for lunch and if anyone should turn up Jules and I can manage. You could always do some exercisin' while you're there,' Edith suggested.

Recently so many other things seemed to have been happening that her working out had been forgotten. Cass chewed at her lip. Though perhaps it had not been forgotten, but was more a case of her preferring not to spend time alone in the villa with Gifford. Because if they were alone she might be stricken with lustful urges towards him.

Or vice versa. Gifford might now be keeping his distance, but his slightly longer-than-necessary looks and a tautness in his body said that he continued to desire her.

'I have to feed Jack,' she said.

'You could feed him at Maison d'Horizon and then exercise. You've no need to change.'

She glanced down at her white sleeveless top and khaki shorts. 'I suppose not.'

'So I'll see you later,' the older woman said, with a grin.

Cass nodded. Steering clear of the villa and its occupant was infantile. She wanted to work out in the gym and she would. If any traitorous urges should arise, they would be quashed. She had will-power. As for Gifford pouncing on her, the danger seemed slight and she would risk it.

'See you,' she replied.

'This afternoon you could take Gifford for a drive around the island,' Edith suggested as she turned. 'A run out'd give you a break from the Forgotten Eden and—'

'Maybe,' Cass said, and headed back towards the kitchen.

As she went in through the swing doors, she gave a twisted smile. Edith seemed intent on pushing her and Gifford together. Should she reveal that he was Jack's father—or had the older woman already guessed? Might that account for why she was keen to matchmake?

She sighed. She ought to let Edith in on the truth, but the truth would include speaking of his objection to long-term parental commitment, and she shied away from that.

Unzipping the baby bag which she habitually carried around, she packed the food and formula inside. Whilst Edith's matchmaking was doomed, her feeding Jack at the villa was not such a bad idea. An awareness of his son's daily activities would draw Gifford in closer, and the closer he could be drawn now, the more chance there might be of him changing his mind and deciding he would like to be close to Jack in the future.

Or perhaps not, Cass thought as she walked up the path to Maison d'Horizon a short while later. Forget the wishful thinking and be realistic. Wise up, she instructed herself. The fact was that here, in the Seychelles, Gifford had nothing much to do. Granted, he continued to make notes for his idiot's guide, but the concept was, basically, a time-filler. Jack rated as a time-filler, too.

When Gifford returned to Boston, he would return to the Tait-Hill Corporation. Once again he would become absorbed in the business—making deals, travelling to oversee various interests, working long hours and giving it all his energy. His son would cease to intrigue, cease to matter.

Cass winced as she strode around to the front of the bungalow. However much it hurt, the brutal truth was that whilst Jack possessed great appeal for him now—it was temporary.

'It's me,' she called, pushing wide the front door which stood half-open.

'In here,' Gifford replied, and she followed the sound of his voice to the living room.

Spacious, and with picture windows which overlooked the garden with its pond and tinkling fountain, the room was elegant. Prints of tropical blooms were pinned on the white walls, bringing the gardeny feel inside. A pale green chenille-covered sofa and armchairs sat on the thick white carpet, while brocade curtains of the same green, intermingled with white and gold, hung at the windows. There was a long, low cherrywood sideboard bearing an exotic arrangement of dried flowers and grasses, and expensive porcelain figurines gleamed in a Camargue display cabinet.

Gifford was sitting on the floor. He wore a grey T-shirt, black shorts and was barefoot. His legs were stretched out, and the baby was attempting to crawl over them. Her heart missed a beat. Gifford's drawn look had gone. In his time on the island, he had already picked up a tan and gained some weight. He looked fit and achingly virile.

'Kidnapper,' she said.

He looked up at her and grinned. 'He seemed as if he wanted some company, and so did I. Watch,' he instructed, and clicked his fingers.

Half suspended over Gifford's damaged leg, Jack heard the sound and looked back. Raising a small hand, he clicked his fingers, too.

Cass burst out laughing. 'I've never seen him do that before.'

'I've just taught him. How many kids of his age do you know who can manage that?' Gifford enquired, sounding every inch the proud father.

Babies were new to him. He had not realised they could give such joy or that they were so absorbing, so uplifting—though Jack was special.

'None,' she said, smiling at him in a moment of shared delight. 'You reckon he's a genius?'

Smiling, he patted the red-dungareed bottom. 'For sure.'

'It's Einstein's lunchtime, so I've brought his food.' Cass tilted her head, her long blonde hair falling to one side. 'Are you going to feed him?'

'Me?'

'Mealtimes can get a bit messy, but he doesn't bite. And, if he should, he's only got two teeth.'

His brow furrowed. 'I've never fed a baby.'

'Now's your chance.'

Gifford considered the idea, then his frown cleared and he nodded. 'When I was in the storeroom the other day I noticed a high chair, so he can sit in that.'

'Wow!'

'This place seems to be equipped for damn near every contingency,' he went on. Lifting Jack off his leg, he held him up to her. 'I'll fetch it.'

Purchased from a top people's store and obviously

unused, the solid pine high chair was wrapped in a sheet of polythene. Cass spread the polythene on the kitchen floor and sat the high chair on top.

'To protect the carpet from fall-out,' she said, fastening the restraining straps around the baby. A bib was tied around Jack's neck, lids prised from the containers and a plastic spoon taken from her bag. She handed it to Gifford. 'All yours.'

Sitting close to the high chair, he held out a spoonful of the pumpkin mixture. Jack opened his mouth and swallowed. And again.

A few mouthfuls on, Gifford smiled. 'I'm getting the hang of this. Aren't I, ragtag?'

The baby grinned.

'I don't suppose you've had second thoughts about— about developing a relationship with him in the future?' Cass asked, his pleasure in the child spurring her into asking the question.

'No.'

His reply was tight, flinty, final.

She was silent for a while, brooding and fuming, then she spoke again.

'Did you go over to the Forgotten Eden in your shorts?'

Gifford nodded. 'Why?'

'Because it's the first time ever. Even if the temperature is in the high eighties and it's as humid as hell you always wear jeans.'

'So?' he demanded, and she heard grit in his voice.

'You wear them because they conceal your leg.'

'My choice of clothing is up to me,' he said curtly.

'If you go out in shorts people may well look, but so what? If it's a problem for them, they're the ones with the disability, not you. Besides, a gammy leg is a ten second wonder. It's no big deal. Was Jack bothered by it just now?'

He swung her an impatient look. 'Of course not.'

'You shouldn't be bothered, either,' she told him. 'Nor should you consider it such a big deal that you use a walking stick and limp.'

'Like a cripple?' he rasped.

'But you are crippled, to a certain extent.'

A muscle knotted in his jaw. 'Thank you for sharing that with me.'

'However, you're not in a wheelchair nor on crutches.'

Gifford shoved a spoonful of mashed pumpkin into the baby's mouth, then turned back to her. His eyes were slate-cold and his expression hostile.

'Is this really necessary?'

Cass kept her gaze steady. She would not be intimidated. She would not back off. It was obvious that Gifford had failed to come to terms with his handicap and needed help. Her feelings for him meant she must give that help—or, at least, try.

'It seems to me that in returning to work too soon you were pretending to yourself that you'd recovered when you hadn't, and in choosing to convalesce on a quiet tropical island far from home you are hiding away. You're refusing to acknowledge your…new situation. You're in denial.'

His fingers tightened around the plastic spoon. 'Claptrap,' he said.

'You have to accept that you'll never be able to do some of the things you used to do as well as you did before your accident—like ski, play tennis, jog. You once talked of getting back to normal, but that—' she indicated his leg '—is normality now.'

'If this is what's called tough love, forget it!'

Cass swallowed down a breath. As he didn't like what he was hearing, so she didn't like saying it. But it needed to be said. As for his reference to her dispensing 'tough love'—the so-apt poignancy of it made her heart ache. Loving him *was* tough.

'But in time your leg will get stronger and you'll still be able to play sports,' she ploughed on.

'What gives you that particular insight?' Gifford asked sarcastically.

'I know you possess the kind of determination and dedication which would ensure the best possible recovery, if you care to motivate them.'

His lip curled. 'If I care to be a plucky little trooper?'

'Yes.'

He slung her a derisive look. 'Thanks for the pep talk. You'll be relieved to hear I'm well aware that there are a lot of folk far worse off than me, and realise I should count my blessings.'

'You should also face the facts. Yes, one aspect of your life has been restricted and naturally you feel a lot of pain, a lot of anger—but it's time to let that go. It's time to capture your demons and move on,' Cass said earnestly.

'It's time you packed in this riveting conversation.'

His voice was quiet, but the tight-lipped precision of his words said that if he had not been feeding the baby he would have raged at her in a fury—or walked out.

'Bravo!' he cheered as Jack ate the last mouthful of his first course. Putting the empty container aside, Gifford filled the spoon with puréed fruit. 'Now for your pudding.'

She frowned. He was moving the focus onto the little boy and evading the issue.

Jack took in the first spoonful, pulled a face as if he had swallowed a wasp and spat the food straight out.

'He usually likes it,' she said as dollops of mango landed on the tray.

'Try again,' Gifford said, and, adroitly scraping a lava of fruit from around the rosebud mouth, he popped it inside again.

This time, Jack ate.

'There're a heck of a lot of things you can do,' Cass continued as the pudding spoon began to move back and forth. 'Life's too short to—'

'Enough!' he rasped, his eyes burning with the savage white flame of anger. 'Leave it alone. If I need advice I'll go to the professionals, not to a homespun agony aunt and do-gooder. OK?'

She nodded. At the rap of his voice, the baby had flinched and was now looking wary. She did not want him to be upset. Besides, her 'pep talk' was clearly a waste of breath.

'If you're willing to give Jack his bottle, I could exercise,' she said.

'Do that,' Gifford replied.

As she made to go, Cass hesitated. 'Edith suggested I take you for a drive this afternoon,' she said, knowing that the woman would be certain to mention it to him. 'But—'

'I'd appreciate a look around the island. What time d'you want to leave?'

'Er—' She had felt sure his irritation with her would have had him refusing. 'Two-thirty.'

'If you fancy a dip, maybe we could finish up at a quiet beach somewhere?'

She nodded. 'I'll ask Edith to recommend one.'

Taking the baby from her, Gifford held him up high in the air. 'Aren't you the smart guy?' he said.

Jack wore a purple and lime-green short-sleeved anti-

UV bodysuit and a purple peaked cap with a flap of cloth which covered the back of his neck.

'A fugitive from the Foreign Legion,' Cass declared, with a tug at the flap.

Grinning down at them, Jack kicked his plump legs.

With Gifford sitting alongside and the baby strapped into his seat in the rear of the Moke, she drove first to the southern end of the island. Taking a road which wound up sharp, steep hills and dropped down in a series of gear-changing, hairpin bends, she brought them to Baie St Anne, a small, tranquil town with a natural harbour which was Praslin's capital.

Here they strolled along the jetty. They admired the yachts which bobbed at anchor, inspected a fisherman's catch of plump red snapper, and gazed out across the blue-green sea to other distant islands.

On their return to the Moke, Cass followed a long, flat road which turned inland to pass through picturesque villages of wooden, corrugated-roofed houses before snaking back to the coast. As they motored along, people often raised a hand in greeting.

They enjoyed a cold drink at a beach-hut café and then, following Edith's directions, turned onto a track and bumped their way—much to Jack's amusement—through a forest to end up at a secluded bay.

As Cass rubbed Jack's arms and legs with suntan milk, Gifford stripped off the T-shirt and jeans which covered his swimtrunks and went into the sea. By the time she stripped down to her black swimsuit and waded in waist-deep, with Jack in her arms, Gifford had powered across the bay and back again.

'I saw lots of fish when I was swimming,' he said, taking Jack from Cass and lowering him half into the clear, warm water. He pushed the baby towards her. 'They swam like this.'

As the little boy chuckled, she turned him around and scooted him back to Gifford. A back and forth game began, with Jack's laughter growing louder and louder.

'Why don't you have a swim while I look after ragtag?' Gifford suggested, when they broke off to watch a shoal of tiny bright blue fish which had appeared beside them.

'Thanks, I will,' Cass said, and waded out deeper.

Although Gifford was a pleasant companion, his attitude towards her had become a touch formal, a touch remote, she mused as she moved her arms in a leisurely breaststroke. A residue of his anger at her pep talk remained.

After swimming and floating on her back, she rejoined him, and they played again with Jack who, laughing and squealing, loved the water. The blue of the sky was fading into the more muted shades of sunset when they walked back onto the sand.

Sitting the baby down, Cass opened her bag and took out a towel. 'Time to be dried,' she told him, then stopped.

Jack had leaned forward onto his arms, eased out the leg which was wedged beneath him and was crawling over the firm sand back towards the sea. It was a tentative, somewhat ungainly crawl, but a crawl nontheless.

'Look at that!' she exclaimed.

Gifford laughed. 'I told you he was a genius.'

'You were right,' she said, gazing happily at the small, moving figure.

He followed, and before the baby could reach the water he scooped him up and into his arms. 'You are a very clever little boy,' he said as Jack gave a protesting wriggle. 'Your mummy thinks so and so do I.'

As Gifford smiled at her, Cass felt an inner glow and, once again, a sense of the three of them as a family. The look in his eyes said that he felt it, too…but then he frowned and turned away.

Closing the ledger, Cass returned it to the desk drawer. The accounts were in order.

'What shall I do now?' she asked Jack, who, after crawling around to explore the office, had eventually wound up on the rug beside her.

It was Sunday afternoon, a week later. Lunchtime cooking duties complete, Edith had gone to visit her sister. Jules had departed for home. And she had completed her bookkeeping.

'You've exhausted yourself,' she said, when the baby gazed dopily up at her. 'So while you have a nap I could sunbathe and read a book or, at long last, I could spring clean the bar. Yes, that's what I'll do.'

She laid him, unprotesting, in his buggy and parked him in a shady corner of the restaurant, then armed herself with cleaning materials. Bottles of rum, port and highly coloured cocktails were removed from the glass shelves which lined the mirrored back wall of the bar. She sprayed on window cleaner and began to wipe.

Unusually, this lunchtime had seen four tables filled. Holidaymakers had reserved two, a local family had celebrated a birthday at another, and Gifford had come over to enjoy a plateful of Edith's tasty fish casserole.

Cass rubbed hard at a stubborn ring of a stain. Whilst his enchantment with Jack meant he continued to be a frequent visitor, his manner towards her remained aloof. Her interference last week still rankled. He refused to acknowledge any truth in what she had said and to forgive her, though he allowed her to use his gym.

Taking a step back, she eyed her reflection in the mirrored wall. For the past seven days she had religiously exercised, and according to Edith's none too reliable weighing scales had lost two more pounds. She turned sideways, her gaze skimming down her figure in the pale blue vest and blue and white Bermudas. Did she look slimmer? Was her stomach flatter? Yes!

When the shelves were clean—and Jack continued to sleep—Cass polished the wall, then began to wipe the bottles, one by one, and replace them. She could not remember exactly which had been where, but Jules could rearrange them later when he came back on duty.

Jules. Her lips moved into a wry smile. The young barman had spent the last ten days attempting to repel the advances of an increasingly ardent Veronica. He had avoided her whenever possible, talked about his numerous girlfriends and begun making repeated—noticeably hopeful—references to how the divorcée would soon be leaving the Seychelles. She was to fly out today.

Veronica had been blithely impervious to Jules's wish to be left alone, and it had not seemed to occur to her that he might not fancy a woman who was some twenty years older.

Yesterday evening—so Jules had revealed at lunch-time—when he had been walking home in the dark, his admirer had drawn up alongside him in her car.

'She'd been waitin' to catch me on my own,' he had told Cass, and grimaced.

'I'll give you a lift,' Veronica had said, and, when he had politely refused her offer, she had stopped the Toyota and got out.

'This is for you,' she had declared, showing him an air ticket. 'So that you can come back to England with me. You needn't worry about getting a job; you can help at the boutique,' she had said, when he started to protest. 'And after a while,' she had added, giggling, 'we can get married.'

At this point in relating his story, Jules had shaken a

disbelieving head. 'The woman is nuts! I told her marriage was the last thing on my mind and there was no chance of me flying back with her. She wanted to know why, and so—Veronica was getting real agitated by this time—I told her that Doris, one of my girlfriends, was pregnant.'

'Is she?' Cass had asked, for it had seemed a possibility.

'No, but I had to say something. Anyway, Veronica declared that it should be *her* who was having my child, climbed back into her car and drove away.' The young man had shuddered. 'The sooner she leaves the island, the safer I'll feel.'

Cass replaced another bottle. The divorcée might have insisted on chasing Jules and was far too self-absorbed, but as she packed her suitcases today she would be feeling lonely. Sad and lonely, Cass thought with a sigh, then heard the tip-tap of high heels. Swivelling, she saw Veronica walking into the restaurant. Talk of the devil!

The redhead wore a tailored calf-length tan suit, black stockings and black high-heeled shoes. A black quilted bag swung on a chain from one shoulder. Her face had been carefully made up and the gold necklace which gleamed at her throat was co-ordinated with her gold drop earrings. Her cases were obviously already packed and she was on her way to catch the inter-island plane which would fly her the fifteen minutes or so over to Mahé, where she would board the jumbo jet to England.

'Is Jules here?' she enquired.

Cass shook her head. 'He left over an hour ago.'

Had Veronica called in to tell him she had come to her senses and to apologise for last night's incident? she wondered. Or might she have intended to make a last-minute plea for the young man to join her?

'Yesterday evening I suggested he fly back with me,'

the new arrival said, coming closer, 'but it was too short notice. I realise now that he couldn't just walk away and leave you in the lurch, and that he has—' a hand was vaguely circled '—other commitments to get out of.'

'Jules doesn't want to leave Praslin,' Cass said gently.

'No?' Veronica looked doubtful, but then her thin face brightened. 'I could buy a house here. Yes, that's what I'll do. I'll buy a house and start up a business, and—'

'You're daydreaming,' she told her.

The redhead pouted. 'I'm not! You don't want Jules and me to—'

She broke off as the telephone which sat on the bar gave a sudden shrill.

'Excuse me,' Cass said, and lifted the receiver. 'Hello?'

'I would like to speak to Oscar,' announced a male voice, with a strong foreign accent. 'This is Wilhelm, an Austrian friend of his.'

'Oscar isn't here,' she said. 'Unfortunately he died a few months ago.'

There was a moment of stunned silence. 'How sad. To whom am I speaking?'

'My name is Cass. I'm Oscar's niece.'

'Then you know what a pleasant fellow he was. Oscar and I had hilarious times together in our younger days. I remember how we travelled to—'

'Goodbye,' Veronica said.

Cass placed her hand over the mouthpiece. The redhead was walking away through the restaurant.

'Goodbye. Safe journey,' she called, but the woman did not look back.

'I visited Oscar at the Forgotten Eden once,' Wilhelm said, into her ear. 'How is the business?'

'It's about to be sold,' she replied, forced to turn her attention back to the phone.

'End of an era. When I stayed with Oscar we...'

Although crackles on the line indicated he was calling long-distance, her uncle's friend reminisced and asked questions for another five minutes.

She must take a look at Jack, Cass thought, replacing the receiver. He had not made a sound for ages. As she wove her way through the tables, her eyes opened wide and she stared. The buggy was empty. Panic leapt, sharp and chill, inside her. Where was her son?

Calm down, she told herself. Gifford would have him. He must. How she had failed to notice his arrival she did not know, but he must have come into the restaurant from the rear, seen her busy on the telephone and taken Jack off to show him the sea or the parrots or... something. That was what had happened, wasn't it? Yes, he had done it before. He had assured her that even if he did need to walk with a cane—his words had been biting—he could safely carry the baby. Cass chewed at her lip. Though before he had asked for permission.

Going to lean over the verandah, she looked around. Where were they? Jack ought to be wearing a sunhat.

'Gifford?' she called, shouting from one side of the restaurant and then crossing to shout from the other. 'Giff?'

When there was no answer, she hurried down onto the beach. It was deserted. Taking the path beneath the trees, she headed for Maison d'Horizon. Although she kept telling herself that there was no need to worry, a mother's need to be reunited with her child and make sure that he was safe quickened her pace. By the time she mounted the steps, she was running.

The gym was empty, likewise the kitchen, but as she reached the study window she saw Gifford. He was sitting at the desk, leaning forward over a portable typewriter and intently typing with his two index fingers. Cass frowned. She could not see the baby.

Backtracking to the kitchen door, she pushed down the handle and dashed in.

'Where's—where's Jack?' she demanded, panting and looking around. 'It would have been polite if you'd asked before whisking him away.'

Gifford stopped typing and turned from the desk. 'I haven't whisked him away,' he said.

'You must've done. Look, if this is some kind of a joke I don't think it's funny. Neither, for your information, do I think much of you making a fuss of him now, when you intend to ignore him in the future. In fact, I think it stinks!'

There was a minuscule silence when he seemed about to answer her charge, but then he decided against it.

'I'm not joking,' he said. 'Jack isn't with me.'

Slippery fingers of fear clawed at her stomach. 'But the buggy's empty.' Her face paled and she looked at him with stricken blue eyes. 'He isn't there.'

'Perhaps Edith's taken him?' he suggested.

'No, she's visiting her sister. She went after lunch and since then I've been on my own. I put him down to sleep in the restaurant while I cleaned the bar. Someone must've sneaked in and—' she put a bemused hand to her brow '—and stolen him when my back was turned.'

Gifford rose to his feet. He had begun to realise that this was a true emergency.

'You didn't hear any noise?' he demanded. 'No sound of a vehicle? You haven't seen anyone?'

'Veronica called in briefly, but apart from that—'

'She has him,' he declared.

Cass shook her head, sending the blonde strands swinging. 'Veronica was going to catch a flight over to

Mahé on her way back home; she'd hardly take a baby along.'

'She would. She's said how much she'd like a child and the woman's neurotic enough to do anything.' Gifford reached for his cane and stepped forward. Gripping her upper arm, he drew her out of the study, through the kitchen and back onto the terrace. 'We'll go to the airstrip. You run on ahead and start up the Moke while I follow.' He steered her forward. 'Hurry!'

CHAPTER SEVEN

Cass ran, retracing her steps down the path to the Forgotten Eden. Charging into her cottage, she grabbed up her bag, located the car keys and sprinted off around to the yard. She had started the engine when Gifford appeared, propelling himself rapidly forward on his stick and breathing heavily. He climbed in beside her.

'Go,' he instructed.

'Fasten your seat belt,' she said, and swung off with a screech of tyres.

'I did warn you about leaving Jack alone with Veronica,' he said as they shot out onto the road.

'I didn't leave him with her! She came into the restaurant and while we were talking the phone rang. When I answered it, she said goodbye and left. Jack was in his buggy and as she passed him on her way out she—' Cass needed to swallow down a rising sob '—she must've picked him up. All it would've taken was seconds.'

Gifford touched her arm. His comment had been unjust, made only because he felt stressed. 'I apologise.'

'How would Jack have travelled in her car?' she said, anxiety churning inside her. 'Veronica doesn't have a child seat and—'

'But her car does have safety belts, so she probably strapped him in between her luggage and padded him around with a coat or something. Jack's a sturdy little guy,' he said reassuringly. 'He'll be OK. He'll cope.'

'I hope so! I pray so. *Please*,' she begged, in a shaky voice.

'How long ago did Veronica call in?' he enquired.

Cass flung the Moke around the perimeter of a pot-hole. 'It can't have been more than fifteen minutes ago. She wanted to speak to Jules,' she said, and as they sped on, passing through Grand Anse, she repeated what the barman had told her about the previous evening.

He frowned. 'Veronica was upset by the claim of his girlfriend being pregnant? Sounds as though he might've triggered off a need for her to take possession of a baby. Even if the baby does belong to someone else.'

'This afternoon she talked about buying a house on the island and moving in with Jules—'

'He'd need to be bound, gagged and dragged there in chains!'

'I told her she was daydreaming and she didn't like it.' Cass shot him a worried look. 'She could've decided to take Jack to get back at me for suggesting that Jules wasn't interested in her.'

'If so, it isn't your fault. Hell, you're allowed to express an opinion. A sensible opinion. But we'll find him,' Gifford said firmly. 'Do you know the time of her flight from Praslin?'

'No, but it might've already left,' she said, and sniffed.

He squeezed her knee, his fingers warm and strong on her bare flesh. 'Be brave.'

'I will,' she replied.

She would not fall to pieces. She could not afford to. The winding country road was quiet—thank goodness—yet she needed to overtake the occasional car, avoid a stray bicycle, be on the alert for pedestrians, cats, dogs and goats.

'If the flight has left, we'll get the police here to ring the police on Mahé,' he said as they barrelled along.

'There's—what—a two hour check-in time for the London flight?'

Cass nodded. 'Something like that.'

'Which means they'll be able to detain the silly, bloody, *thieving* woman in Departures.'

'But suppose she slips on board an earlier plane which is bound for somewhere else? Veronica could fly to a number of different places, to different continents, and vanish. Or she could skip the airport and vanish into Mahé. With Jack!' she said, and her stomach cramped.

'Mahé is small enough for a lone female who is carrying around a baby, but has no food or clothes for it, to be quickly traced. Especially a female who has a compulsion to chatter, like her.'

'I suppose so,' Cass agreed.

'She seems to have taken Jack on the spur of the moment and hasn't thought things through,' he went on. 'She doesn't have a passport for him, yet she'll need to show one to get through Immigration at Mahé so she'll be stopped there. She won't have a chance of—'

Gifford broke off. They had reached the fenced boundary of the airfield, and diagonally across the expanse of grass which was centred by the airstrip a De Havilland Twin Otter was parked alongside the small terminal building. The closing of a luggage hatch indicated that the aircraft was almost ready for take-off.

'Is that the Mahé plane?' he enquired.

'I think so, though we'd better check.'

Her foot pressed down hard, Cass drove the Moke down the length of the fence, swung onto a short drive and came to a halt beside the terminal. As they flung open their doors and clambered out, they heard the noise of an engine rumbling into life.

'Oh, no,' she said, in a stricken voice.

'There's still time,' Gifford declared, and, taking a

tight grip on his cane, and ushering her with him, he hobbled speedily towards the building.

They went directly into a waiting room which served as both the arrivals and departures hall. Here a young woman in the uniform of an airport official was standing beside an open door, looking out onto the airstrip.

'Is that the Mahé plane?' Gifford demanded.

'Yes, sir. Our regular service.'

'Would you ask your air-traffic control, or whoever's in charge, to tell the pilot to cut his engine and remain stationary?'

'Cut the engine?' she repeated, as if he were crazy.

'Immediately,' he rapped. 'It's essential.'

'You were hoping to catch that flight?' She shone him a soothing smile. 'Sorry, sir, every seat is full, but even so I couldn't ask—'

'We're too late. It's leaving,' Cass said, gazing in dismay as the small De Havilland began to roll off slowly along the grey ribbon of tarmac. Pain tightened like a vice around her chest. 'Jack's on that plane and—' her voice broke '—I might never see him again.'

'I'll stop it. I'll get him back,' Gifford vowed, and launched himself past the young woman, out through the door and onto a paved area.

Employing his cane as extra propulsion, he limp-swung rapidly across to the strip. He shouted and waved his arms, but he was towards the rear of the aircraft.

As the airport woman looked on in bemusement, Cass followed. 'It's no use,' she called. 'No one's seen you and they can't hear—'

Her words died. Gifford had flung down his cane and started to run. As the De Havilland continued to move slowly forward, he was loping unevenly alongside, shouting for it to stop and waving like a madman. He wore shorts, and his legs moved like pistons, one noticeably thinner than the other.

She frowned. Whilst impulse might have started him running, it could only be sheer will power which kept him going. And the pressure on his injured leg must be tremendous. He could be wrecking the surgeon's painstaking work and causing even greater permanent damage.

'What does that guy think he's doin'?' enquired a policeman, walking up to stand beside her. Pushing back his cap, he scratched his grizzled grey head. He supposed he ought to set off in pursuit, but he was a good few pounds overweight, and there was no point risking a heart attack. 'Only a lunatic runs in this heat.'

'Our son's been kidnapped and he's trying to halt the plane,' Cass told him, and swung round. 'Did you notice whether a red-headed woman wearing a tan-coloured suit and carrying a baby got on board?'

The policeman nodded. 'The *bébé* kept making a grab for her earrings and she didn't like it.'

'I hope he rips off her ears! The baby is my son, Jack, and she's taken him, and—'

'Your fella's been successful,' the policeman interrupted, and when she turned she saw, to her surprise, that the aircraft had begun to slow.

Picking up his discarded cane on the way, she sped along to where Gifford was standing, gasping for breath, as he waited for the plane to come to a halt.

'Are you OK?' Cass asked.

'I—I think so,' he managed.

'I didn't hold out much hope of you stopping the plane, but—'

'Nor me. Get the steps!' he called as the De Havilland came to rest, and a man in overalls dutifully began to wheel some over.

'That was some run,' declared the policeman, who had followed her. 'Your wife must be pleased she has an athlete like you around.'

Wife? She waited for Gifford to correct the officer, but he was too busy panting to reply.

'I am,' she said, deciding that now was no time to embark on an explanation of their relationship.

Gifford indicated the plane door which was in the process of being released from the inside.

The steps were pushed into place and the door pulled open. When she saw Veronica standing there with Jack in her arms, Cass felt a huge, rolling rush of relief. The baby, who was yanking at one of the redhead's drop earrings, looked lively and cheerful.

Gifford placed an arm around Cass's shoulders. 'He's safe.'

Looking at him, she gave a watery smile. 'Thanks to you,' she said, and sped up the steps to retrieve her son.

'Let's get this straight,' Gifford said, frowning. 'You took Jack because he smiled at you?'

Veronica nodded. 'He was waking up and he smiled and lifted his arms—as if he wanted to go with me, though now I think he was just stretching—and, well, he seemed to care about me when no one else did.'

'So you decided to abduct him?'

'It wasn't a conscious decision, I just got carried away. I'm sorry,' she said, sniffing back tears, and then continued. 'He was fine in the car; he laughed every time we went over a bump. But on our arrival at the airstrip—'

'Jack cried?' Cass demanded, when the redhead broke off to frown.

Although her nerves were still ravaged and her heartbeat had yet to steady, the baby was at ease. She looked down at where he rested on her knee, contentedly suck-ing his thumb. There was no evidence of tears, but per-haps earlier he had sensed danger, felt frightened and had sobbed.

'On the contrary, he was boisterous,' declared the el-derly Frenchwoman who had been sitting beside Veronica on the plane. 'He was what I believe, in English, you call "a tyke".'

They were in an office at the terminal. When the policeman— who had been joined by a second, younger officer—had conferred with the pilot it had become clear that the flight had been aborted not because of Gifford's efforts—the pilot had been unaware of him—but thanks to the Frenchwoman. Apparently she had heard Veronica's worried admission of kidnap and had promptly reported it to the cockpit.

And when the policemen had announced to the curi-ous passengers that they were taking the redhead away for questioning the Frenchwoman had insisted she could give pertinent information. So the plane had departed without her, too.

'While we were standing in the queue to check in, the infant was continually squirming and wriggling and making a grab for things,' the old lady explained, in her no-nonsense manner.

'He even dribbled on my suit,' Veronica said.

Gifford arched a brow. 'You didn't go a bundle on that?'

'Well—no. This suit is from an exclusive collection by a famous Italian designer. It cost the earth, even wholesale.'

'You hadn't realised that babies can be a bit of a hand-ful?' Cass enquired.

The redhead shook her head. 'Jack's always been good. So cute. But today he just wouldn't be still.'

'Maybe he didn't approve of being abducted and decided to put you through hell,' Gifford suggested.

Veronica looked shamefaced. 'Maybe.'

'And maybe you should've thought about what the hell you were putting Cass through!' he continued.

'I should—and, like I've said, I'm sorry.'

'Sorry?' His laugh was harsh. 'Can you imagine how Cass felt when she realised her child had vanished? Are you aware of the distress, the *terror* which you caused?'

The redhead sniffed again. 'I am, and I regret it with all my heart.'

'Have you kidnapped a child before? In your own country?' demanded the younger policeman, who was keen to take charge of the proceedings and conduct his own interrogation. Weeks often went by with nothing of significance to report, and today's episode made an exciting change.

Veronica recoiled in horror. 'Good heavens, no!'

'Is that the truth? We can check to see if you have a criminal record,' he warned her.

'It's the truth, I swear,' she said earnestly. 'I've never, ever been in any kind of trouble.'

'Until now,' the older policeman declared.

'I took Jack on impulse, but I soon realised my mistake. Please forgive me,' she said, and splashy tears began running down her cheeks.

'When I sympathised over how the infant was bouncing around, she told me he didn't belong to her,' the Frenchwoman said, speaking to Cass and Gifford. 'She confessed she'd abducted him, but vowed that the minute we landed on Mahé she would phone you, explain where he was and arrange to return him.'

Veronica nodded vigorously. 'I was going to catch the next flight straight back here.'

'It sounds as though you must've been relieved when

the plane stopped and you were able to get rid of him,' Gifford said drily.

'She could not get rid of him quickly enough,' the old lady declared. 'She is not of a motherly disposition. Are you?'

The redhead frowned. 'No. I'm a businesswoman.'

'And Jack's cured you of hankering after a baby?' Cass enquired.

Veronica dabbed a handkerchief at the streaks of black mascara which had formed on her cheeks. 'For always,' she said, with feeling.

'You gave his parents a nasty shock,' the younger policeman said sternly.

She looked puzzled. 'Parents?'

'Mr and Mrs—?' The policeman referred to Gifford.

'Tait,' he provided.

'Although Mr and Mrs Tait have been reunited with their son, I must arrest you and—'

'A-arrest me?' the redhead said shakily.

'Is that necessary?' Cass enquired.

She had been expecting Veronica to argue against the 'Mr and Mrs', but she was obviously too engrossed in her own problems to query the attachment. As for Gifford, he seemed content to remain silent and, indeed, to promote the idea.

'An arrest would be normal procedure,' the policeman replied, 'though it depends on whether or not you wish to press charges.'

Leaning towards Gifford, she spoke in a lowered voice. 'If Veronica's arrested, she might be put in prison. I wouldn't want that. She didn't cold-bloodedly plan to take Jack, and she was going to return him, and—'

'You're too soft-hearted. Personally I'd have the woman locked up and the key thrown away for all time,' he said, into her ear. 'But a case could drag on for months, so—' He straightened. 'We don't want to take the matter any further,' he informed the police officers.

The two men exchanged reluctant glances. They had been looking forward to the chance of appearing in court and having their part in the case reported in the local newspaper.

'Then it's over and done,' the older man declared.

'Thank you, thank you so much,' Veronica said, weeping again. 'You're all so kind and understanding. I deeply regret my sin and I shall remain forever in your debt.'

The Frenchwoman raised her brows at this somewhat dramatic pronouncement, then looked out at the airstrip where another Twin Otter aircraft was coming in to land.

'If we take that plane, perhaps we shall reach Mahé in time to catch our scheduled flights,' she said hopefully.

One of the policemen nodded. 'I'll ring the airport, madam, and ask for you to be given priority.'

As a subdued Veronica went with the old lady to wait for the plane to disgorge its passengers and accept the next batch on board, Cass hoisted Jack up in her arms. Together she and Gifford returned to the Moke.

'How does your leg feel?' she enquired, anxiously eyeing him as he limped on his cane beside her.

'Achy and weak, as if I've just run a marathon.'

'You almost did. Suppose we call in at the hospital on our way back through Grand Anse?' she suggested.

'No need.'

'But a doctor could check you out.'

Gifford shook his head. 'I'll live with it for a while,' he said firmly.

'I was amazed when you flung away your stick and galloped off,' Cass said as she buckled Jack into his seat and climbed inside.

'Not as amazed as me,' he remarked drily, lowering himself down into the Moke beside her. 'The plane was still moving slowly, and I thought that if I could some-how manage to run across in front of it—'

'Run in front?' she protested. 'But if the pilot didn't see you they'd have needed to scrape you up, one inch thick, from the runway.'

He grinned. 'Not such a good idea, huh?'

'A crazy idea,' Cass said, smiling, then she made a strangled sound and launched herself into his arms. 'I was so scared,' she sobbed. 'Scared for you and scared for Jack and scared for me.'

As the tears which she had been fighting back for so long streamed down her cheeks, Gifford held her close. He stroked her back and kissed her hair and comforted her. And when the baby looked worried he said soft, comforting words to him, too.

Eventually, Cass blew her nose and wiped her cheeks.

'Better now?' he asked as she settled back into her seat.

'Much better,' she said, and switched on the ignition. 'A few minutes before you set off on your marathon you'd been telling me how Veronica couldn't take Jack out of the country because she didn't have his passport,' she reminded him as she swung the Moke out onto the road. 'You were insisting she'd be detained on Mahé, then—whoosh!—off you raced to retrieve him.'

'I saw how distressed you were and decided I wouldn't let her remove him from this island. Not if I could help it. I'd been convinced I'd never run again, but—' Arching an arm along the back of his seat, he smiled at Jack. 'You and your mother sure got me go-ing.'

'You must've been close to breaking the world record for the thousand-metre sprint,' Cass said teasingly, then frowned. 'I hope the pounding you gave your leg hasn't done any more damage.'

'If it has, it has—but it'll take a day or two to tell. You're a dead loss,' Gifford went on, speaking to the baby again. 'You get kidnapped, but do you weep bitterly and scream? Do you hell—you enjoy it!'

Jack clapped his hands.

'You might think you were clever,' Cass said, giving him a laughing glance through the rear view mirror, 'but Veronica thought you were a complete pain.'

'Thank the Lord,' Gifford said heavily.

She nodded soberly. For the rest of the journey, she gave silent thanks for the baby having been a nuisance, for the redhead realising her error, but most importantly for Gifford coming to the rescue. Veronica's insistence that she would have returned Jack had seemed sincere, yet if he had been docile...

As they turned into the drive to the Forgotten Eden, they saw Edith walking ahead of them. Wearing a navy and white dress and with a white straw hat on her glossy dark head, she was returning from visiting her sister.

Cass hooted the horn. 'I'm glad we're back,' she said, when Edith waved. 'If she'd arrived and found the place deserted, she would've been worried.'

'Where've you been?' the older woman enquired curiously as they climbed from the Moke.

Cass reached inside to unstrap the baby. 'We were retrieving Jack.'

'Veronica had kidnapped him,' Gifford said.

Edith's eyes widened into two round saucers. 'Kidnapped?'

'But Gifford ran like the wind and the plane stopped—'

'Courtesy of the Frenchwoman,' he inserted.

'And we got Jack back.'

'What plane? Which Frenchwoman?' came the per-
plexed query.

'Why don't we go inside and tell you the whole
story?' Gifford suggested.

Edith nodded, then cast him a look. 'You ran like the
wind because…you are Jack's papa?'

'I am,' he said. 'But you knew that.'

She gave one of her rich chuckles. 'I've known for a
while. He's the spittin' image of you and, besides, you'd
never drool over some other man's child like you drool
over him.'

Amusement glinted in his grey eyes. 'I drool?'

'Shamelessly. And you drool over Cassie here, too—
when she's not lookin'.'

'Do I?' he muttered, and frowned. 'Running is thirsty
work. Do you think I could have a beer?'

'Coming up,' Cass said smartly, and, passing him the
baby, she wheeled away into the kitchen.

If Edith considered that Gifford drooled over her, she
might well have noticed her drooling over him. But she
did not want her to say so.

Cass yawned. After a day when she had expended so
much nervous energy and been wrung out by so many
swooping emotions, she felt exhausted. Stepping out of
the bath, she dried herself and pulled on the oversized
white cotton T-shirt which she used as a nightgown.
Although it had yet to reach ten o'clock, she was going
to bed.

Quietly opening the door to the small second bedroom, she peeped inside. Jack's lively mood had persisted for the rest of the day. He had refused to settle
until mid-evening, but now he lay in his cot, on his back
and with his arms crooked above his head, fast asleep.

As she looked at the small, peaceful figure, a warmth curled around her heart. Her son was safe.

Cass was heading for her own room when she heard a soft tap-tap on the front door. She sighed. This would be Edith.

After the busier than usual lunchtime, there had been no dinner reservations, and no casual customers had arrived. As she had attempted to coax Jack to go to sleep, Edith and Jules had sat in the restaurant, discussing Veronica and voicing heartfelt thanks that the redhead was now winging her way home.

'Looks like nobody's coming, so Jules has left,' Edith had told her, when Cass had gone across to report that, at last, the baby had fallen asleep. 'I wondered if Gifford might want a meal, but that run of his must've tired him out.'

She had nodded. 'He'll be resting.'

As she went to open the door now, Cass frowned. The oven had been switched off and the food placed in the fridge, so it was too late for dinner. But latecomers could have appeared requesting drinks at the bar; no doubt Edith now required her assistance. She tucked a strand of hair tiredly behind her ear. Whilst turning down trade went against the grain, this was one occasion when she would have gladly told customers to beat it.

But it was Gifford who stood on the doorstep.

'What's the matter? Is your leg hurting? Do you want me to run you to the hospital?' she demanded, instantly alarmed.

'No, thanks. My leg still aches, but that's all. And look—' he held up both hands '—no stick. I decided that as long as I use it I'll need it. So I'm going to have a shot at walking without it.'

'Now? Only hours after running your marathon? And

you came here in the dark. You might've fallen,' Cass
protested.

'I didn't. I used a torch and was careful. Though if I
do fall I can stand up again. I'm here because there's
something I need to say.' His eyes dropped to her out-
sized T-shirt. 'But if you're going to bed—'

'Not just yet,' she said, too grateful to him for retrieving the baby to turn him away. 'Come in.'

'Thanks.' Gifford walked through the tiny vestibule
and into the living room.

Lit by the diffused golden glow from a table lamp,
the room had whitewashed walls, faded yellow cotton-
twist rugs on a sanded wooden floor, and was sparsely
furnished with a brown batik-upholstered cane sofa, two
armchairs and a low glass coffee table. Filmy white mus-
lin curtains covered the window which looked onto a
small, unevenly paved patio at the rear. Although the
curtains, rugs and furniture were clean, they had seen
better days.

Gesturing for him to be seated on the sofa, she sat
down on a chair. 'What is it you need to say?' she enquired.

'I need to explain why, when you asked if I was willing to be around Jack as he grew up, I said I didn't think
it was a good idea.'

Cass gritted her teeth. It was obvious that today's
scare would have made him think more deeply about
their son and his relationship with him, but she was too
tired to listen to his reasoning and to his excuses.

'I'm sorry, but I don't—' she started to protest.

'It was because I'm—' the word seemed to stick at
the back of his throat before he forced it out '—disabled.'

'Jack won't care about that,' she said impatiently.

'Maybe not, but *I* cared. I thought about him being

saddled with a father who limped, who couldn't play a regular game of baseball and teach him other sports like dads are supposed to, and—and it threw me.' Gifford frowned, disgusted with himself. 'I decided it'd be better if I stayed away and spared him the disgrace.'

She shook her head. 'Giff, he—'

'Hear me out. I felt that if I couldn't be a proper father to Jack—a perfect father—I wouldn't be a father at all. And yet no fathers are perfect. Mine certainly isn't,' he said grimly. 'But then two things happened. First, what you said last week about me ceasing to wallow in self-pity and getting off my butt—'

'I didn't say that,' she objected.

'It was the gist. What you said set me thinking.'

Cass shot him a suspicious glance. 'It did?'

'Initially I told myself you were wrong, you hadn't got a clue about how I felt, you didn't understand, et cetera. But gradually I began to wonder if you might be right. Remember I said you were allowed to express an opinion to Veronica?'

She nodded. 'A sensible one.'

'I realised that you were expressing a sensible opinion with regard to me and how I was handling, or mishandling, my disability.'

'What was the second thing which happened?' she prompted, when he stopped and frowned.

'This afternoon, I ran. For the first time since the accident I forgot about my leg—I forgot about the injustice of being crippled—and I ran.'

'In desperation and through sheer strength of mind,' Cass said.

'Yes, but I managed it and I can manage a lot more. I can stand on my own two feet, even if sometimes it is shakily,' he said wryly. 'This evening I've been recovering and rethinking. I accept I'll never be as agile as I

used to be. I recognise that—' he swung her a look '—as
you said, I'll always be disabled to a certain extent. But
it doesn't stop me being a father to Jack and I *want* to
be a father to him. I want to be around as he grows up.
Is that OK?'

Joy lifted Cass out of her chair and onto the sofa to
sit beside him. 'Yes. Oh, Giff, yes.'

'Thank you,' he said. 'Before I was loaded down with
thoughts of everything I couldn't do, but now—' Taking
hold of her hand, he raised it to his lips and kissed the
sensitive inside of her wrist where the pulse beat. 'Now
I know that anything is possible.'

'And life looks good again?'

Gifford smiled, his eyes warm on hers. 'Life looks
very good,' he murmured, and leaned forward.

A vague awareness of their words echoing those
which they had spoken over eighteen months ago, when
they had first made love, made Cass pause. Hesitate. He
was going to kiss her, but his kisses were seductive.
They could lead into lovemaking. She wanted him to
make love to her. After all the trauma of the day, she
craved the closeness and the comfort, but—

'I care about you,' Gifford said, as if he sensed her
doubts and needed to banish them.

'Um—ditto,' she said.

Smiling, he brushed his lips across her lips. 'So?'

As his mouth covered hers, Cass tossed caution aside.
Wrapping an arm around his neck, she moved closer.
Her lips parted. Tongue grazed against tongue. The kiss
deepened. Although a small voice warned that she could
regret it in the clear light of day, she was responding to
her emotions and to the language of her body which said
she needed him.

All tiredness had gone. Now adrenalin surged,
threaded through with desire. Cass stirred restlessly. Her

breasts felt heavy against the fine cotton of her T-shirt. A quicksilver ache throbbed in the pit of her stomach. Her skin shimmered with anticipation.

'Silk,' Gifford said, sliding his hands up the smoothness of her thighs. 'You're made of silk.'

He took hold of the hem of her T-shirt and pulled it up to her waist, her breasts and off over her head. Casting the garment aside, he gazed at her, his grey eyes heavy-lidded and slumberous. Then he reached out his hands and took hold of her breasts, weighing them in his palms.

'Glorious,' he murmured, and eased her back against the cushions. Burying his face into the angle of her neck, he kissed the soft skin. 'Mmm, you smell as good as you look.'

Cass smiled. 'It's baby moisturising bath gel.'

'Plus the fragrance of you,' he said throatily.

He fondled her breasts, his thumbs stroking lazily across her nipples until she arched her back, bit at her lip and whimpered. His hands trailed down. As if re-learning the erotic pleasures of her body, he slid his fingers over her stomach, her hips, and to the triangle of pale hair.

Cass whimpered again.

'Do I need to take precautions?' he enquired.

She shook her head. 'I'm on the pill.'

'Good. Though I am prepared.'

Raising her hands, she steered him back from her and focused. 'You came prepared? You were so certain I'd…succumb?' she protested.

Gifford grinned. 'Let's just say I knew that if I succumbed you would. And the chances of me succumbing were high. But I didn't want us to make a second mistake.'

'You are so—so arrogant!' she declared.

'It's not arrogance, it's realism. You and I were always going to make love again. It's unavoidable. It's destiny.' Easing her down onto the cushion again, he kissed her. 'Yes?' he enquired, a little while later when they came up for air.

'Yes,' Cass agreed meekly.

As he skimmed his fingertips over her nipples, she strained closer, pressing the swollen curves into his palms. Then she was pulling at the buttons on his shirt, opening it, stroking her breasts against his chest.

'God, Cass,' he said, in a strained voice. Rising to his feet, he put his arm around her waist and shepherded her through the half-open door of her bedroom and inside. 'Help me,' he said, his hands going to the belt of his jeans.

Together they removed the rest of his clothes, then he lowered her onto the bed. His hand closed possessively over the cluster of blonde curls which grew at the junction of her legs, then slowly, slowly cruised up her body, over her waist, over the narrow ribcage, and to the fullness of her breasts. And when he had touched her his mouth followed.

Cass trembled. As his fingers had seemed to know exactly where to caress, so his lips knew just where to linger. He pleasured her for a long, delicious time, then moved up beside her on the pillow. He kissed her again, his manhood burning hot and hard against her thigh.

Sliding a hand down between their bodies, she touched him. Now it was his turn to tremble.

Gifford fought to keep himself from taking her too quickly, too greedily. He had messed up their relationship in the past, but he was not going to make a mess of their lovemaking. He wanted it to last. He wanted to take her to the limits and give her the deepest, wildest satisfaction.

Cass grew bolder, her fingers curling around the velvety muscle.

'Honey,' he muttered, and submitted to her touch until he felt his control begin to falter.

He touched her intimately, his finger probing the moist, secret crevice of her body, and she arched up against him. He touched her again, sensuously rubbing, and she tightened, shuddered, exploded.

'I'm sorry,' she said. 'It's been so long since—'

Gifford smiled. 'It'll happen again.'

He slid into her, his weight wedged between her thighs. He moved his hips and thrust deeper. She gasped. Her breath was coming quickly, their bodies rocking in the rhythm of love. Perhaps it was because she had slept alone for so long, but their intimacy seemed twice as thrilling, twice as wonderful, more spiritual than anything she had ever known before. Or did she feel like this, she wondered, because she knew that she loved him?

'Now,' he said, his voice harsh and guttural. 'For God's sake, Cass, now.'

He thrust again, and, in a fusing of flesh and a spiralling of giddy emotion, she surrendered completely.

'I needed you so much,' Gifford said as they lay together afterwards in the lazy languor which followed lovemaking. His mouth curved into a grin. 'The other day I damn near took you on a table in the restaurant.'

'Too public,' Cass said.

'Where's your spirit of adventure?' he demanded, then his grin faded. 'Ever since we met again I've wanted to make love to you, but I was frightened that the thought of my leg might intrude and spoil things. Afraid that *I* might think about it, dammit!' he rasped, in abrupt, self-chastising anger. 'It made me feel…inadequate.'

'You, inadequate? Never. And did you think about your leg just now?'

'Not once.'

'Neither did I.' She smiled at him across the pillow. 'I was too busy thinking about…other parts of you. Parts which are in good working order.'

Taking hold of her hand, he slid it down his body. 'Magnificent working order,' he said.

Cass grinned. 'I can't disagree with that.'

'And?'

'You're insatiable,' she said.

'I haven't made love for a heck of a long time,' Gifford protested.

'Not since your accident?'

'Not since I last made love to you.'

She looked at him in surprise. 'That's eighteen months ago,' she protested.

'Doesn't do much for my virile man-about-town image, does it?'

'Not a thing.'

'But I never came across another girl who appealed to me as much as you did. No other girl came anywhere near.'

Cass smiled. She liked what she was hearing. 'You weren't tempted to ring Dial-a-Date or place an ad in an ''encounters'' column?' she asked, her eyes sparkling.

'Bachelor, late thirties, non-smoker, with his own apartment and own teeth, wishes to meet slim blonde with view to fun and games? Nope.' He drew her closer. 'However, I have no intention of remaining celibate for that length of time again.'

'I have no intention of allowing you to remain celibate for that length of time again,' she said, suddenly serious, suddenly desperate for him.

Their mouths met and, like drunkards, they drank in

each other. Her hand stroked him, sure and strong, and as his need began to howl he rolled her beneath him. He entered her, pushed up on his arms, and lowered his dark head to suck hard on the pointed tips of her breasts.

'I can't wait so long this time,' he warned.

'I don't want you to wait,' she replied, her hips rocking against his.

At the tug of his mouth on her breast, she cried out, and as Gifford felt the moist convulsion of her thighs he allowed himself to follow.

'Doesn't it bother you that our son is a love-child?' he enquired as they lay in bed together some time later. 'Don't you mind that he's illegitimate? Maybe it's not regarded as so much of a stigma these days, but—'

'I mind,' Cass interrupted. 'I mind a lot.'

'Me, too. So why don't we consider a joint future?'

She eyed him warily. 'What does that mean?'

'Marriage.'

Surprise had her sitting upright. 'You're suggesting we become Mr and Mrs?' she enquired.

Gifford nodded. 'Like the police officer believed earlier. Problem?' he asked, when she frowned at him.

'A big one,' she said, and pulled up the sheet to cover her breasts. His gaze had, she noticed, wandered down. 'To quote your own words, you have a "dread of being tied down". You're "not cut out for domesticity".'

His eyes darkened. 'You have a good memory.'

'It was a memorable moment,' she countered.

He sat up, pushing a pillow behind him. 'Suppose I said I've changed my mind and that, all of a sudden, domesticity seems extremely attractive?'

'I'd take it with a pinch of salt. I'd also say that the "all of a sudden" is relevant and advise you to think again.'

'There's no need.' His expression was level and grave. 'Please, Cass, will you marry me?'

Her heart seemed to stop and start again. Once upon a time, she would have willingly sold her soul to hear those words. She would have felt that all her dreams had come true. But now...

Gifford's aim was to give Jack his name, publicly acknowledge that he was his father and make him respectable. It was an admirable aim and she was touched. Yet although, earlier, he had said he cared about her, he had not mentioned love. Cass bit hard into her lip. Love was deeper, stronger and more intense than caring. Love mattered.

All current evidence indicated that if they married they would get along well together, and the sexual side promised to be great. Plus, Jack would grow up within a proper family. She wanted that. And yet...

And yet she would always be aware that love did not feature in Gifford's equation. It was an awareness which seemed destined to eat away at her peace of mind, erode and, in time, destroy.

Or would it? Her thoughts fluctuated wildly. As Gifford loved the baby, might he not grow to love her? He could, she argued with herself, so shouldn't she take the chance? She longed to take it.

But he might meet another woman, fall in love, but decide to stay with her out of duty, she thought, her imagination firing. Would she be able to bear that?

'No,' Cass replied.

He shoved his hair off his brow. 'You prefer to go solo?'

'I do, but—but I'd like us to still be friends. OK?'

He nodded. 'OK.'

'I also want you to come and see Jack whenever you wish.'

'Thanks.' Turning back the sheet, Gifford reached for his clothes and swiftly dressed. 'Good night,' he said.

Cass gave a tight smile. She had just refused to marry a man who was kind and supportive, with buckets of integrity—and a man whom she loved.

'Good night,' she replied.

CHAPTER EIGHT

JULES was late.

The tables had been set and, with much toing and froing, a cold buffet laid out on a long blossom-bedecked trestle-table. Hot dishes waited, ready, in the kitchen. Cass looked at her wristwatch. The tour party was due to arrive at any moment, but what had happened to the barman?

The party was, so the coach company had rung to advise earlier that morning, larger than usual. A sleek white cruise ship had anchored off the island at Baie St Anne and several passengers had applied to join the excursion. This meant that while Edith worked flat out behind the scenes Cass and Marquise would need to dash around like demented robots in the restaurant. Keeping pace replacing buffet dishes and clearing away the used crockery was going to be difficult enough, without them also needing to dispense the drinks.

As she checked, yet again, that Jack was obligingly deep into his middle-of-the-day doze, the tour party coach pulled into the yard.

'It looks as though Jules has overslept,' she said, speaking to Marquise who had already begun to peel off the cling-film covers from salad bowls.

The teenager nodded and made a face. 'But why must he choose today of all days to catch up on his beauty sleep?'

Cass was waiting to greet the holidaymakers when she suddenly tilted her head and listened. There was the low rumble of a male voice in the kitchen.

162

'About time!' she exclaimed thankfully, and sped through. 'You're cutting it fine—' she started to protest, then stopped.

The voice she had heard belonged to Gifford, who was standing talking to Edith.

He grinned. 'Hi. I went swimming earlier and when I was on the beach I smelled curry, so I've come over to see if I can entice Edith to save me a plateful.'

'And she said you could have as many platefuls as you wished?' Cass enquired.

Edith laughed. 'You guessed.'

Enticing the ever-grateful Edith would have been easy, she thought wryly. But then enticing any female would have been easy for Gifford. Dressed in a short-sleeved checked shirt which was open to show his strong, smooth throat and a tuft of dark hair, and wearing chamois-coloured shorts which fitted neatly around his backside, he packed a powerful masculine punch.

If he should decide to try, there seemed little doubt that he could entice the proverbial birds from trees, mermaids from rocks and—her heartbeat juddered—her back into bed.

Cass tugged fretfully at a wisp of blonde hair. Whilst she could not, in all honesty, regret their intimacy—it had been too blissful for that—she would prefer to avoid a repeat performance. Further lovemaking could only mean a further shredding of her heart and a further whack at her vulnerability. No, thanks.

She had spent all of yesterday on edge, wondering if they might, somehow, end up hotly entwined again, but her worrying had been unnecessary. Whenever Gifford had been around—he had taken Jack for a walk and eaten dinner at the Forgotten Eden—his attitude towards her had been amiable. Period. She had fallen asleep feeling relieved that he had agreed with her request that they should just be friends…yet had also felt irrationally disappointed.

'Where's ragtag?' he enquired.

'He's fast asleep, safe and sound, in his buggy behind the screen in the restaurant, with Marquise acting as bodyguard.'

'You check on him every thirty seconds now?'

Cass grinned. 'Every fifteen.'

'Thought so.'

'How's the leg today?' she asked.

Gifford bent and straightened his knee. 'All recovered.'

'You're looking very alive this morning,' Edith told him.

'I feel it,' he replied.

Since being released from hospital, it had become his habit to spend the evenings sipping Scotch and staring into space. But for the past few nights he had drunk mineral water, listened to music and read. The records were big band Cole Porter and the book was a Somerset Maugham, left in the villa by some previous tenant. Neither would have been his choice, yet the evenings had passed with surprising ease. And now, when he woke up in the morning, he felt an optimism and a renewed sense of energy.

Gifford frowned. Last night, his reading had been abandoned for thoughts of Cass. She was the only woman he had ever asked to marry him—the only woman he had ever wanted to marry—and she had turned him down flat. Nice going, Tait, he thought.

His spur-of-the-moment proposal had been a surprise for them both. Matrimony had never held any attraction for him. OK, his view was jaundiced, but the idea had filled him with horror. Yet now the more he thought about it, the more it appealed. He liked being with Cass and the baby. He liked the idea of them living together as a family. He had felt pleased and proud when the policeman had assumed that they were married.

He pushed his hands into his pockets. When he had indicated there was no problem about them being friends—just friends—he had lied. He wanted more than friendship. Much more. He wanted—no, he *craved*—her heart, her soul, her body…

'I thought you were Jules,' Cass said now.

'He hasn't turned up?'

'No.' She grimaced at the shuffle of footsteps entering the restaurant. 'And today we're feeding the five thousand and we need him to serve the drinks.'

'Suppose I do it?' Gifford suggested.

Her eyes widened. 'You?'

'I can pour a beer as well as the next guy.'

'Well, yes, I suppose so, but—'

'But what?' he enquired.

But your leg could give way when you're carrying a tray and you might go sprawling, Cass thought. Then people would rush to help and fuss and sympathise, and you'd hate it.

'You don't know how much the various drinks cost,' she said feebly.

'I'll check the prices on the wine list and if I need any help I'll ask you,' he replied, and jerked a thumb towards the restaurant. 'Scoot.'

As she hurried out to welcome the customers and direct them to their tables, Gifford went behind the bar. He undertook a speedy assessment of the stock, spread the wine list out on the counter, then armed himself with a ballpoint pen and notepad.

'Would anyone care for a drink?' he asked, re-emerging to smile at the occupants of the nearest table.

Although jugs of iced water were provided, the local

Seybrew lager proved to be popular with the men of the group, while the women tended to choose soft drinks or wine. As Cass kept the supplies of salads and hot food flowing, and later helped Marquise carry out platters of caramel bananas, home-made lime sorbet and coconut tart, she was aware of Gifford ferrying trays of glasses and bottles back and forth.

As she made one of her repeated checks on Jack, she cast him an anxious glance. There was an ocean of difference between him saying he had accepted his disability and putting that acceptance to the test before a restaurant full of strangers. Please don't let him fall, she prayed.

'Look, Mummy, look!' a piercing voice suddenly shrilled. 'You must look!'

The shout came from a little girl. Aged around six, pretty with fair curls and wearing flowered leggings and T-shirt, she was the only child in the party. Earlier she had called out to marvel at a gecko which had been clinging to the trunk of a palm, and again when a black flying beetle had buzzed in like a bomber plane, and everyone had stopped talking, turned to see and indulgently smiled.

Once more she was calling and pointing, but this time her focus was on Gifford as he delivered beers to a nearby table.

'Mummy, look at that man's leg,' she demanded.

Cass went cold. The group had fallen silent. Gifford had tensed.

'Yes, dear,' mumbled the child's mother, a plump, mousey-haired young woman. 'Now eat your ice cream.'

'But it's—'

'Becky, be quiet,' growled her bespectacled father.

'But it's a yucky leg!' the little girl pronounced, loudly and clearly.

Cass's stomach churned. With heads craned and eyes peering, the entire restaurant was looking at Gifford who had straightened to stand upright. Becky's parents seemed as if they would dearly love to gag their garrulous daughter, but Cass wanted to strangle her. She also longed to put a protective arm around Gifford's shoulders and lead him away.

'Yucky, and yet magic,' Gifford said, with a smile.

The little girl looked up at him, down at his withered limb, and back up again. 'What do you mean?' she asked suspiciously.

'It can tap dance all on its own.'

'How?'

'Like this,' he said, and, putting down the tray he carried, he tapped his toe and then his heel.

He was wearing canvas leather-soled shoes, and as he moved his foot he rapped out a sound on the floorboards. Clip-clop.

Cass relaxed. He did not need her protection. He could cope wonderfully well on his own.

Becky giggled and grinned up at him. 'It is magic,' she said.

'Perhaps you have a magic leg, too,' he told her. 'Want to try?'

'Yes, please,' she said, slithering down from her chair to stand beside him.

As Gifford continued to toe and heel, the little girl attempted to copy him. At first she struggled, but all of a sudden she picked up his movement and rhythm.

'I do! I have a magic leg like yours!' she cried, delightedly clip-clopping.

People laughed and offered encouragement. Other feet began to tap. Someone whistled. 'Eat your heart out, Gene Kelly,' a man shouted.

Gifford continued the performance for a couple more

minutes, then he bent and spoke to his partner. As they stopped to take grinning bows, everyone in the restaurant burst into loud applause.

Cass clapped and thankfully smiled. He had turned what had been shaping up to be a very awkward moment into a time of fun.

'Not only do you take over as barman, you also provide the cabaret,' she said, grinning at him as they waved off the tour party half an hour later.

'I thought a chorus of ''On The Good Ship Lollipop'' might've gone down well,' he said, straight-faced, 'only I couldn't remember the words.'

'''Dream Lover'' would've gone down better,' she said, recalling how the female members of his audience had seemed particularly entranced. 'The tips were larger than usual, so how about dancing for the next group?'

'And be spotted by a talent scout, offered a million-dollar contract and asked to star in my own show on Broadway?' Gifford turned down his mouth. 'Not my scene.'

She heaved a noisy sigh. 'Some people have no spirit of adventure.'

'Some people are desperate for their plate of curry,' he told her, and headed for the kitchen.

Jack had been washed and was sitting in the bath, playing with a yellow plastic duck while Cass shampooed his hair.

She was kneeling, gently sluicing away remnants of bubbles with warm water, when the doorbell buzzed. Her pulse rate quickened. Earlier Gifford had asked what time she usually bathed the baby, so this would be him.

'Come in,' she called, and a few seconds later he appeared in the doorway.

'OK if I watch?' he asked.

She indicated the space beside her at the deep white old-fashioned enamel bath. 'Have a ringside seat.'

He bent and, gripping her shoulder for support, eased himself down onto his knees. He smiled.

'Thanks,' he said, his hand lingering.

The touch acted like a green light to her nerves. It made her aware of being with him in the cottage. It reminded her—sharply—of the sexual attraction which existed between them. It ignited an erotic charge which seemed to flare through her body.

'The bottom of the bath's slippery and occasionally Jack topples over,' Cass said, edging away, 'so would you keep a hold of him while I fetch his clothes?'

He released her to place a large, steadying hand behind the baby's back. 'Will do.'

As she opened the drawer and took out a fresh white sleepsuit, her brow crinkled. Had Gifford come simply to see their son being bathed or might he also be here because he wanted to make love to her again? His smile and his touch hinted that way.

Cass gnawed at her lip. She did not want them to make love. Yes, she did, she acknowledged, but the more intimacy they shared now, the worse she was destined to feel when they went their separate ways.

When she returned, Gifford was swooshing Jack up and down the bath, and as he shot through the water the baby was flinging up his arms and giggling.

'This is boys' play,' Gifford told her.

She knelt down. The tableau they presented—the fond father with his happy son—clutched at her heart. Perhaps she should say she had changed her mind and that she would marry him. Jack's life would be so much richer and…perhaps Gifford's lack of love for her did not matter. Cass gave her head a little shake. She was deceiving herself.

Splash! The baby smacked his hands down flat on the surface of the water and a fountain sprayed up into the air. It hit Gifford full in the face and drenched his shirt.

'You little monster!' he exclaimed, veering back and blinking.

She laughed. 'It's called a learning experience.'

'Who for, him or me?'

'Both,' she replied, grinning.

She handed him a towel and, as she took control of the baby, he dried himself.

'How about drying Jack?' she suggested.

Gifford nodded. 'But you'll have to tell me how to do it.'

'OK. First…'

A few minutes later the baby was lying, dried and smelling of talcum powder, on a thick towel on the bath-room floor. He kicked his chubby legs and smiled up, as if he felt secure in the knowledge that the two of them would always be there for him, together. Cass's heart clenched. Wrong, she thought.

'Now you put on his nappy,' she said.

Gifford swung her a look. 'I do?'

'You have to complete the whole rigmarole.' She handed him a disposable nappy. 'Are those cold beads of sweat which I see starting from your brow?'

'Dead right,' he said, but he fastened on the nappy and, with some fumbling, dressed the baby in his sleep-suit. 'Bedtime,' he decreed, when Jack yawned.

'Not until he's had his bottle.'

There was another enormous yawn and his eyelids fell.

'Too late,' Gifford said.

'Looks like it,' she agreed. 'All the sliding up and down in the bath must've worn him out, but if he wakes up hungry in the middle of the night I'll—'

'Turn a deaf ear?'

'Bring him round to you to feed,' Cass responded, and carried the sleeping child off to his room.

As she laid him down, kissed him and drew up the side of the cot, Jack never stirred.

'Out for the count,' she reported, coming back into the living room. She frowned. Gifford was bare-chested. 'Your shirt was too wet to wear?'

He shook his head. 'No.'

'So?'

Reaching out a hand, he linked long fingers with hers. 'I thought that if I stripped off you might be turned on and feel inclined to strip off, too. And then—' He grinned and drew her closer. 'Are you turned on?' he asked, his voice lowering into a husky purr.

Cass swallowed. Because the Seychelles were close to the Equator, every day the sun set at around six-thirty and it was dark by seven. Twilight lasted for a preciously short time, but it was twilight now. The rich golden glow from a sinking sun filled the room, gilding the smooth skin of his shoulders, the planes of his chest, glinting amongst the whorls of coarse dark hair. Hair which had scoured against the tips of her breasts when they had made love.

'A—a little,' she said breathlessly.

A grin travelled along his lips. 'Liar.'

'OK, a lot!'

'And you're cross with yourself for being so damned pliable?'

She frowned. 'Yes.'

'Don't be. It works two ways,' Gifford said, and bent to kiss her on the mouth. 'Come with me.'

In her bedroom, he peeled off the rest of his clothes and, amidst more kisses, he started to undress her. Her shirt was removed and Cass shimmied out of her shorts.

Now all she wore was a low-cut white lace bra and G-string briefs.

He looked at her, his grey eyes heavy with desire. 'I thought I could make myself stay away from you, but I can't,' he said, and stepped nearer.

His hands slid beneath her arms and around her back, releasing the bra hooks which lay between her shoulder-blades. The straps were lifted forward and her breasts released. Casting the bra aside, he cupped the full, high curves. He savoured their silky warmth, then skimmed his palms up over the taut honey-brown nipples.

Cass shuddered out a breath.

As she stood rigid, he stroked and fondled her breasts. And when they were swollen, the nubs straining with need, he clasped her ribcage. He drew his hands down, over the slenderness of her waist and her hips, hooking his thumbs into the elasticated strings of her briefs and drawing them down, too.

'You never did wear sensible knickers,' he said.

She managed a smile. ''Fraid not.'

'You're shaking,' Gifford murmured.

She laid her head on his shoulder. 'So are you.'

'True, but I'm an invalid so I'm allowed to shake.'

'Excuses, excuses.'

'I don't fool you?' he asked, his fingers doing outrageous things to the hot, damp crevice of her flesh.

'Not—not in the least,' she said raggedly.

As the white lace scrap of her briefs joined the bra on the floor, he steered her down with him onto the bed. He kissed her. Hard. The muscle of his tongue drove into her mouth and moved, exploring, tasting, until she was giddy and gasping for breath.

Cass clung, intoxicated by the pressure of his lips on hers, their taste, and drugged by the closeness of his firm male body. He brought his hands to her breasts again, moulding, caressing, pinching. She cried out, aware of hurtling towards a deep, engulfing chasm, and her body bucked against his.

'My lusty lady,' Gifford murmured.

Now his mouth was on her breasts. He licked, he sucked on the sensitive peaks, he savoured. When she felt the soft bite of his teeth on the moistened flesh, she whimpered and arched her spine.

Cass pressed her thighs into his thighs. His arousal was hard and heated. She reached down to caress him with slow fingers.

'Still shaking,' he said throatily.

'You…or me?'

'Both.'

She stroked him and, easing back, moved down his body so that her mouth could caress as her fingers had caressed.

'Sweet mercy, Cass,' he muttered, his voice thick and heavy.

He submitted to her pleasuring for long, tense, blissful moments, and then he drew her up. She put her hand on his hip, pushing him flat and kneeling astride him.

Gifford grinned. 'Be gentle with me,' he said.

She eased herself onto him, moving and swaying. 'But not too gentle?' she asked.

'Right,' he said, on a groan.

Cass bent, rubbing her breasts against his chest, her nipples teasing on his nipples in a way which excited them both. She kissed him, her mouth hungry, and teased him with her breasts again.

As need built, she sat up, her hips locked to his and her spine straight. Gifford raised his hands to fondle her swollen breasts until her breath came in low, throaty moans and her head turned from side to side in desire.

'Please,' she gasped. 'Giff, please.'

Holding her hips and lifting his thighs, he drove deeper. As he stroked a fingertip over her pulsing beak of secret flesh, sensations whirled. She moaned and, throwing back her head, closed her eyes. He drove into her again. Stroked again. Then he was forcing her to the edge of the chasm and over…tumbling her down, down, down into sweet, dark oblivion.

'Was that somebody wanting to reserve a table?' Edith enquired, walking into the restaurant the next morning.

'No.' Cass looked down at the telephone which she had just been using. 'I was speaking to the airline about my return flight,' she said, and gave a strained smile. 'I've decided to go home at the weekend. On Saturday.'

The older woman frowned. 'So soon?'

'It isn't soon really. I've been here for over six weeks. I said I'd stay until the Forgotten Eden was sold, and the deal'll be complete in two days, on Friday,' she rattled off. 'Friday's your last day of trading, so you don't need me any longer.'

'Not *need*, but I was hoping you'd be here for my move into the house.'

Cass flashed another strained smile. She had guessed Edith had this in mind and she felt such a heel.

'I'm sure you and your sister'll manage fine and—I ought to get back.'

'What about Gifford?' the older woman enquired.

'We shall keep in touch and he'll fly over from the States to see Jack from time to time, and—' she gave what was intended to be a casual shrug '—that's it.'

'What does he think about you leaving?'

She frowned. 'He doesn't know. I keep meaning to tell him, but I haven't got around to it yet. I thought that maybe we should put a notice in the local paper advising that the Forgotten Eden is changing hands,' she continued, becoming businesslike. 'We could also place a board at the end of the drive advising any passers-by that the restaurant will be shut after Friday, though re-opening under new management later. Shall I do that?'

Edith nodded. 'Please.'

Cass rang the newspaper office on Mahé and arranged for an announcement, then she found an old menu black-board and wrote out a 'closing down' announcement in chalky capital letters.

'You're happy to look after Jack while I take this along to the road?' she asked Marquise, who had fin-ished her cleaning and was playing with the baby.

The teenager grinned. She liked babies and small chil-dren. She had heard about a well-off family on the other side of the island who were in need of a nanny and she was going to apply for the position.

'Sure.'

Carrying the blackboard, Cass set off down the drive. Although she felt bad about deserting Edith, she had decided she must leave the island as soon as possible. She needed to put space between herself and Gifford.

Yesterday evening they had made love and she had no doubt that, this evening, he would come to her cot-tage and the same thing would happen again. Again he would stay the night. All he needed to do was kiss her—or take off his shirt!—and any hard-won resistance which she had managed to assemble instantly crumbled.

She frowned. She had been putting off telling Gifford of her intention to leave because she was afraid that he might attempt to persuade her to stay. Given her current state of mind, she could easily submit to his persuasion, and if she did she would be offering herself up to an even greater emotional battering. But she must tell him, soon.

Cass propped the blackboard up against the trunk of

a tree. Before she left, they needed to agree on the sum which he would pay towards Jack's upkeep. It would also help if she had some idea of how often Gifford intended to visit his son. Her heart twisted. Which meant how many times a year she would need to see him.

Once she was free from his presence, she would be able to reassemble her composure and start thinking straight, and so when they met in future she would be able to resist him. She would, she assured herself. Her biddableness was a temporary blip.

She had swivelled to retrace her steps when she saw Gifford walking towards her along the drive. In the two days since he had abandoned the use of his stick, his stride had already strengthened and his limp did not seem quite so severe.

'What do you think you're playing at?' he shouted.

Cass looked down at the blackboard. 'I was giving a warning about the restaurant closing. Do you think it's premature and that I might put off any would-be customers?' she called.

'It's not premature, and if folks realise this is their last chance to enjoy Edith's cooking they might all rush here for a final meal,' he said as he reached her. 'What I meant was, what the hell do you think you're playing at, trying to sneak off on Saturday?'

'Edith told you?' she asked.

'She did.' Gifford glared. 'She did the decent thing.'

Her chin angled upwards. 'I was going to tell you.'

'When?'

'Soon,' Cass said. 'I wasn't trying to sneak off.'

'No? You hadn't planned to keep quiet about your departure until the last minute, pack quickly, say goodbye and go?'

Her cheeks burned. The idea had occurred to her, but she'd rejected it. 'Of course not,' she declared, and with her head held high she marched past him and back off along the drive.

'You and I need to sort out a few things,' Gifford said, coming alongside her.

She nodded. 'Like how much you should pay towards Jack. I've worked out how much I spend on him each month, on…'

As they returned to the Forgotten Eden, she gave him details of her usual budget and suggested a sum.

'OK?' she enquired.

'Later,' he said dismissively, and ushered her into the restaurant where Marquise was crouched amongst the tables, playing peek-a-boo with a giggling Jack.

The teenager looked up. 'Hello.'

'Would you babysit for, say, half an hour?' Gifford enquired. Taking rupee notes from the pocket of his shorts, he placed them on a table. 'I'll pay you.'

Marquise smiled as she eyed the money. 'I can stay for as long as you want. For one hour or two. All day.'

'Jack will need to be fed at around twelve,' Cass said.

'I can feed him,' the girl offered eagerly.

Gifford shook his head. 'Thanks, but we'll be back before then. If he should cry, we're up at the bungalow,' he said, and, taking hold of Cass's arm, he steered her out of the restaurant.

'There's no need to manhandle me!' she protested as he steered her across the lawn. 'I'm not going to run away.'

'Not until Saturday?'

'I'm not running away then,' she said. 'It's just time for me to go.'

He flung her a glowering look. 'Is that right?' he muttered, but he released her.

When they reached Maison d'Horizon, he led the way into the living room.

'Another matter which we must sort out is your visits,' Cass declared, sitting on the sofa. 'How often—?'

'I don't want to visit,' he said, frowning down at her. 'I want to live with you.'

'Live with me?' she echoed. 'You mean…permanently?'

'Of course permanently,' he rasped. 'You've said you don't want to marry me, but how about us living together? We get along fine and the sex is fantastic. But rapport and animal passion apart—' Raising his hands in a gesture of frustration, Gifford pushed them roughly back through his hair. 'I love you, dammit!'

Although his words provoked a leap of emotion inside her, she refused to be poleaxed or grateful or tricked.

'Since when?' she enquired. 'Since you fell head over heels in love with Jack?'

'Long before that. When we first met in London.'

Cass shook her head. 'Our history doesn't quite back that up,' she said crisply. 'If you recall, you ditched me.'

'And you were hurt?' he asked.

'I was. Desperately,' she said, deciding that this was a time for honesty. 'I may've acted blasé at the time, but it was an act.'

Gifford sat down at the other end of the sofa. 'I wondered, but I couldn't be sure. I ditched you—' he winced at the word '—because, although we'd only known each other for a matter of weeks, I was aware of getting in deep. Very deep. It scared the sh— It scared me,' he settled on.

She frowned. 'So you cut and ran?'

'Yes. And I blew it. I mentioned my father once and his marriages and divorces. Growing up, I saw what a mess he made of his relationships—the pain he caused, to his wives and to his kids.'

'You have brothers and sisters?' Cass asked, before he could continue.

'I have a younger half-brother and two half-sisters. Whenever we meet we always seem to wind up talking about Pop and how he deceived us all.'

'Deceived?'

He nodded. 'My father is an appealing guy—well-mannered, fine-looking, humorous. He gives the impression that he's interested in you and he cares, but the only person he's ever cared about is himself.'

'He didn't care about you—or your brother and sisters?' she protested.

'Didn't give a damn. Like most kids, I idolised my father,' Gifford carried on. 'When I was young I felt sure he loved me, too, but he only ever saw me—saw any of his kids—because our mothers insisted on it. And they needed to apply a lot of pressure. It was a long time before I realised that, and when the truth dawned—' He pressed his lips together, recalling his teenage angst. 'It wrecked me.

'However,' he continued, 'when Pop was married to my mother and he complained of her restricting his life, of how he felt smothered, and later, when he accused other women of doing the same thing, I guess I believed him.'

'And became anti-marriage?'

Gifford frowned. 'No and yes. On the one hand, whenever I met couples who were happily married I envied them. I also consider that marriage should be for ever and have old-fashioned values, like believing in fidelity and responsibility and having a duty to be there for your kids. On the other hand, I was scared of being trapped.' He gave a twisted smile. 'Plus, deep down, I think there was a fear that I might turn out to be as feckless as my father.'

'So, rather than take a chance, you preferred to go it alone?' she said.

'Yes. But going it alone can be lonely. I figure one reason why I immersed myself so deeply in work was to cut down the number of hours I had to spend on my own.'

'You've never lived with anyone?' Cass enquired.

'Once a few years ago, but the girl kept nagging me to marry her and so eventually I cut and ran. After that I vowed I'd never live with anyone again.'

'But you've changed your mind?'

He nodded. 'When I ended our affair and went back to the States I moped around, missing you like hell, which is why I agreed to Imogen's invitations. I had some cock-eyed idea that going out with her might stop me from thinking about you.'

'It didn't?' she said.

'No way. I'd decided I would never see you again,' Gifford went on, 'but I couldn't get you out of my mind. I said I telephoned you because I felt bad about the way I'd ended our relationship—that was true, but I also rang because I wanted to discover whether or not you had a new boyfriend.'

'Why?'

'Because by that stage I'd decided that if you were unattached I'd fly over and ask if we could start over again. But Stephen indicated that the two of you had become a couple so I stayed put.' He wetted his lips. 'During my months in hospital, I spent a lot of time thinking about how I'd loved you, how I knew we could've had a great relationship and how I'd screwed up.'

'Loved me. Past tense?' Cass queried.

'It seemed that if you were involved with Stephen I was wasting my time.' His dark brows lowered. 'I told myself I was over you, but I was deceiving myself. I figure that, subconsciously, I chose the Seychelles as a place to convalesce because the islands had a connection with you.'

'But you didn't think I'd be here?'

'Never. And meeting you threw me. Then, when it seemed as though you'd had a child with Stephen…'He blew out a breath. 'That hit so hard. But I do love you, and perhaps, in time, you'll love me.'

She smiled. As he had been talking and explaining, happiness had been growing inside her. At first, it had been a cautious trickle, but now it was surging through her veins like warm wine and singing in her head.

'You think I might?' she said.

'It's possible. Cass, you wouldn't sleep with me unless you cared something for me,' he said earnestly, 'and if we live together—'

'No, thanks.'

'You don't want to live in the States? OK, we'll live in England. We'll live here.' He threw up his hands. 'We'll live wherever the hell you want.'

'I don't want to live with you.'

'You think I could be a bad bet, like my father? Cass, I'm not,' Gifford insisted. 'I know now—'

'I don't think that. I know that you care—really care—about people. About Jack. About me.'

'So why…?' he said, in confusion.

'I don't want to live with you, I want to marry you because I love you, too,' Cass told him.

He grinned, a slow, lopsided grin. 'You do?'

'I've loved you since we first met.'

'Thank God,' he said, and he kissed her. It was a long, needy kiss, but when it ended he pulled back to frown. 'Why did you refuse to marry me?'

'Because you never mentioned that vital word "love".'

'You didn't give me time,' he protested. 'Like you said, I proposed on the spur of the moment. OK, it was kind of…bald, but I guess I thought you knew I loved you. Even so, I was working up to a declaration of undying devotion when you said no. I ought to have persevered, but you sounded so damn anti, and I felt wrecked and—' He lost patience with himself. 'Cass, I love you now and for always,' he said gravely, and kissed her again.

'Shall we go and tell Jack that, from now on, he'll have a full-time mummy and daddy and be legitimate?' she asked as they came up for air.

'After we celebrate.'

'With champagne?'

Gifford grinned. 'That comes later.'

'You have something else in mind?' she said, her blue eyes shining.

'Something which is far more exhilarating and has been known to make us both shake.' Rising, he pulled her to her feet and wrapped his arms around her. 'How about it?'

Cass smiled up at him. 'You're irresistible,' she said.

CHAPTER NINE

'GIVE me one last hug,' Edith appealed, smiling at Jack, and he launched himself from Gifford's arms into hers. She held him close. 'I shall miss you, *bébé*.'

'You'll see him again in about two months' time,' Cass reminded her.

'At your wedding,' Edith declared. 'I can't wait.'

Gifford grinned. 'Nor me,' he said. 'We'll call and tell you the date as soon as it's fixed.'

'I'll book my flight straight away,' Edith assured him. She kissed the baby. 'And I'll see you when your mama and papa come back to stay at Maison d'Horizon for their honeymoon. You're a whizz at crawling now, so will you be walking by then?'

'Could be,' Cass said.

'And before we know it you'll be dating girls, hanging out at discos and wanting your own car. A top-of-the-range Ferrari,' Gifford said, tickling him.

Jack chuckled.

They were at Praslin's airstrip. Their luggage had been checked onto the flight to Mahé prior to them travelling on to London, and as they waited to board the small plane Edith had launched first into thanks for all the help they had given her and was now moving into her goodbyes.

Five weeks ago, Cass had cancelled her hastily arranged flight home.

'I've paid the rent on the villa for two months,' Gifford had said, 'so why don't we stay here and have a vacation?'

She had grinned. 'Yes, please.'

So as Edith had moved out of the Forgotten Eden she and Jack had moved into Maison d'Horizon. The first couple of weeks, when they had helped install Edith and her sister into their house, had been busy. Gifford had hung pictures, fixed shelves and tidied the garden, while Cass had generally fetched and carried. But, ever since, they had been on holiday.

They had sailed to several of the other islands, including the untouched and breathtakingly beautiful La Digue. They had spent a few days in a hotel on Mahé, where they had boarded a semi-submersible boat to enjoy the underwater glories of the coral reef, walked along picture-postcard bays with Gifford carrying a sun-hatted Jack in a backpack, hired a car which had enabled them to call in at potteries, art galleries and a sculptor's studio, and buy a stained-glass fish from a local craft shop.

After so much cleaning and waitressing, Cass had enjoyed the chance to relax—and Gifford had abandoned his idiot's guide.

'Got better things to do,' he had decreed.

Back on Praslin, they had swum and sunbathed and talked for hours over long, lazy meals. And, amidst all the swimming and sunbathing and talking, they had made love. Such wonderful love.

'First you're going to stay with Cassie's father?' Edith said, recapping on their plans now.

'So that I can ask him for his daughter's hand in marriage. And about time,' Gifford said, with a grin. 'While we're there, we shall organise the wedding.'

'Then we remove my belongings from Stephen's apartment, store them at my father's house, and fly over to Boston,' Cass went on.

'Where you'll stay in Gifford's apartment,' the older woman said.

He nodded. 'We shall live in Boston after we're married, so we're going to look for a house to buy on the outskirts of the city.'

'With a garden for Jack to play in when he's older,' Cass said.

'Then we'll return to England, walk up the aisle and fly back out here for three weeks,' he concluded.

'And after your wedding I'll stay on with Cassie's father—it's very kind of him to invite me—and come back a week later.' Edith gave a satisfied smile. 'I'm so grateful to you for negotiating that wage with Kirk,' she told Gifford, reverting to her thanks again.

After the sale of the Forgotten Eden had gone through, Kirk Weber had asked whether Edith would consider working as a weekend cook at the restaurant, and if Jules might be interested in continuing there as barman.

'I've been told about the delicious food which Edith produces,' he had said, speaking to the three of them. 'And there was a woman staying at Club Sesel recently who talked loud and long in praise of your barman.'

'A redhead?' Cass had asked, with a grin at her companions, and Kirk had nodded.

'What do you reckon to working here at the weekends?' Gifford had enquired, turning to Edith.

'I'd like it,' she had replied.

'You'll pay her the same wage as you pay your chefs?' he had asked the South African.

'International rates? I don't—'

Kirk had protested, but Gifford had argued and won through. When Jules had said he would be pleased to carry on, Gifford had managed to get him a rise, too.

As the passengers began walking out to board the Twin Otter, Edith kissed the baby again and passed him back to Gifford. She hugged Cass close.

'Have a safe journey,' Edith said, suddenly tearful.

'We will,' she replied.

Gifford bent to kiss the older woman's cheek. 'Take care.'

Waving goodbye, they climbed up the steps and found their seats. A few minutes later, they were flying high over the sea.

Gifford smiled at Cass who held the baby on her knee.

'Bachelor, late thirties, with his own teeth, has met slim blonde and is going to marry her,' he said. 'He will live with her and their children—'

'Children?' she cut in.

'I reckon we should provide Jack with a brother or a sister in a couple of years' time. Don't you?'

'Good idea,' she agreed.

'He will live with her and their children for ever and ever in perfect bliss.' He grinned at the baby. 'What do you think about that, ragtag?'

Raising his hands, Jack snapped his fingers.

'He thinks it's a cinch,' Cass declared, laughing.

Gifford took hold of her hand. 'Me,too,' he said, and smiled into her eyes. 'Me, too.'

MILLS & BOON®

Next Month's Romances

♡

Each month you can choose from a wide variety of romance novels from Mills & Boon. Below are the new titles to look out for next month from the Presents™ and Enchanted™ series.

Presents™

THE DIAMOND BRIDE	Carole Mortimer
THE SHEIKH'S SEDUCTION	Emma Darcy
THE SEDUCTION PROJECT	Miranda Lee
THE UNMARRIED HUSBAND	Cathy Williams
THE TEMPTATION GAME	Kate Walker
THE GROOM'S DAUGHTER	Natalie Fox
HIS PERFECT WIFE	Susanne McCarthy
A FORBIDDEN MARRIAGE	Margaret Mayo

Enchanted™

BABY IN A MILLION	Rebecca Winters
MAKE BELIEVE ENGAGEMENT	Day Leclaire
THE WEDDING PROMISE	Grace Green
A MARRIAGE WORTH KEEPING	Kate Denton
TRIAL ENGAGEMENT	Barbara McMahon
ALMOST A FATHER	Pamela Bauer & Judy Kaye
MARRIED BY MISTAKE!	Renee Roszel
THE TENDERFOOT	Patricia Knoll

H1 9802

Available from WH Smith, John Menzies, Martins, Tesco and Asda

One special occasion—that changes your life for ever!

Everyone has special occasions in their life. Maybe an engagement, a wedding, an anniversary...or perhaps the birth of a baby.

We're therefore delighted to bring you this special new miniseries about times of celebration and excitement.

Starting in March 1998 in Enchanted™ we then alternate each month between the Presents™ and Enchanted series.

Look out initially for:

BABY IN A MILLION
by Rebecca Winters in March '98 (Enchanted)

RUNAWAY FIANCÉE
by Sally Wentworth in April '98 (Presents)

PARTY TIME!

How would you like to win a year's supply of Mills & Boon® Books? Well, you can and they're FREE! Simply complete the competition below and send it to us by 31st August 1998. The first five correct entries picked after the closing date will each win a year's subscription to the Mills & Boon series of their choice. What could be easier?

BALLOONS   BUFFET   ENTERTAIN
STREAMER   DANCING   INVITE
DRINKS   CELEBRATE   FANCY DRESS
MUSIC   PARTIES   HANGOVER

S	O	E	T	A	R	B	E	L	E	C
T	E	F	M	U	S	I	C	D	D	H
S	U	I	V	Z	T	E	Y	R	A	A
N	E	N	T	E	R	T	A	I	N	N
O	B	V	E	R	E	H	K	N	C	G
O	J	I	F	O	A	L	R	K	I	O
L	M	T	F	V	M	P	U	S	N	V
L	P	E	U	Q	E	N	Z	S	G	E
A	W	G	B	X	R	C	T	B	Y	R
B	F	A	N	C	Y	D	R	E	S	S

C8B

Please turn over for details of how to enter...

HOW TO ENTER

Can you find our twelve party words? They're all
hidden somewhere in the grid. They can be read
backwards, forwards, up, down or diagonally. As
you find each word in the grid put a line through it.
When you have completed your wordsearch, don't
forget to fill in the coupon below, pop this page
into an envelope and post it today—you don't even
need a stamp!

Mills & Boon Party Time! Competition
FREEPOST CN81, Croydon, Surrey, CR9 3WZ
EIRE readers send competition to PO Box 4546, Dublin 24.

Please tick the series you would like to receive if you
are one of the lucky winners

Presents™ ❑ Enchanted™ ❑ Medical Romance™ ❑
Historical Romance™ ❑ Temptation® ❑

Are you a Reader Service™ Subscriber?   Yes ❑   No ❑

Mrs/Ms/Miss/Mr ....Intials ....
(BLOCK CAPITALS PLEASE)

Surname..

Address ....

....

....Postcode...........................

(I am over 18 years of age)   C8B

One application per household. Competition open to residents of the UK
and Ireland only. You may be mailed with offers from other reputable
companies as a result of this application. If you would prefer
not to receive such offers, please tick box. ❑

Closing date for entries is 31st August 1998.

Mills & Boon® is a registered trademark of
Harlequin Mills & Boon Limited.

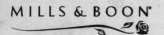

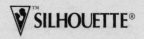

SPECIAL OFFER £5 OFF

We have teamed up with Flying Flowers, the UK's premier 'flowers by post' company, to offer you £5 off a choice of their two most popular bouquets the 18 mix (CAS) of 10 multihead and 8 luxury bloom Carnations and the 25 mix (CFG) of 15 luxury bloom Carnations, 10 Freesias and Gypsophila.

All bouquets contain fresh flowers 'in bud', added greenery, bouquet wrap, flower food, care instructions, and personal message card. They are boxed, gift wrapped and sent by 1st class post.

To redeem £5 off a Flying Flowers bouquet, simply complete the application form below and send it with your cheque or postal order to; **HMB Flying Flowers Offer, The Jersey Flower Centre, Jersey JE1 5FF.**

FLYING FLOWERS

Beautiful fresh flowers, sent by 1st class post to any UK and Eire address.

ORDER FORM (Block capitals please) Valid for delivery anytime until 30th November 1998 MAB/0198/A

Title .... Initials .... Surname ....

Address ....

.... Postcode ....

Signature .... Are you a Reader Service Subscriber **YES/NO**

Bouquet(s) **18 CAS** (Usual Price £14.99) **£9.99** ☐   **25 CFG** (Usual Price £19.99) **£14.99** ☐

I enclose a cheque/postal order payable to Flying Flowers for £ .... or payment by

VISA/MASTERCARD ☐☐☐☐☐☐☐☐☐☐☐☐☐☐☐☐ Expiry Date .... / .... / ....

PLEASE SEND MY BOUQUET TO ARRIVE BY .... / .... / ....

TO Title .... Initials .... Surname ....

Address ....

.... Postcode ....

Message (Max 10 Words) ....

Please allow a minimum of four working days between receipt of order and 'required by date' for delivery

You may be mailed with offers from other reputable companies as a result of this application.

Please tick box if you would prefer not to receive such offers. ☐

Terms and Conditions Although dispatched by 1st class post to arrive by the required date the exact day of delivery cannot be guaranteed. Valid for delivery anytime until 30th November 1998. Maximum of 5 redemptions per household, photocopies of the voucher will be accepted.